For a man who knows his monsters, Shane D. Keene

CHAPTER ONE

Even the Scottish whisky can't stop the nightmare from coming. And believe me, they have some pretty incredible shit here. The locals drink it like water, but I'm not a local.

I may have been here for five years, but they'll never accept this American interloper. Fine by me. I realize I'm just a transient, albeit one that's been here for a handful of years. When the time comes, I'll be happy to leave the Highlands forever. A girl can only take so much sourdough and tartan.

Hmm, but I will miss the scenery. So pretty out here. Well, when it's not foggy, overcast, or raining. And the Scottish men, nothing to complain about there, though I wish I could understand them a little better. I have a terrible ear for accents and sometimes I can't believe we speak the same language. I was barely able to understand what went on in the movie *Trainspotting*. This is a whole new level.

I'm up and sweating and can't catch my breath.

Again.

Is it technically a nightmare when the thing that wakes you up in the dead of night is a memory?

Not that it matters.

Nightmare…memory…either way, I can never get a full night's sleep.

I slip my legs out from under the covers, grab the glass of tepid water I keep next to my phone charger, and gulp it down. When it comes, I sweat enough to soak through my clothes.

Years ago, my simple solution was to sleep in the nude.

It didn't work out. Changing sheets is a hell of a lot harder than slipping on a fresh pair of panties, sleep shorts, and a T-shirt.

The spare clothes are neatly folded on the floor by my feet. I stand, stretch, get down to my birthday suit, pat myself down with a towel, and get dressed.

The radio is still on, some late, late night call-in show hosted by someone with such a thick accent, I can barely understand what the hell he's talking about. Like I said, I'm Scottish tone deaf.

Snapping the radio off, I collapse back into bed.

The good news is, the nightmare never comes twice.

The bad news is, falling back to sleep is never a guarantee. It's almost four in the morning.

Early to bed, early to rise.

I went to bed at midnight. Not sure that constitutes early.

I close my eyes, the remnant of the nightmare – memory – still playing like an old filmstrip as the heat from the projector bulb rapidly melts it away.

It was 1995. Shania Twain had exploded on the music scene. I couldn't stop playing her CD. The fact that it pissed off my twin brother Austin was just a bonus. He was all grunge, all the time, back then.

We were camped right where my RV sits now. Me, Austin, Mom, and Dad.

My father had been downsized by the genetics company where he'd worked for almost twenty years. They gave him a goodbye package that left us flush with cash. No tears were shed. He was a scientist toiling away for a corporate entity. He'd felt he'd sold his soul for long enough.

So he took us out of school and we headed for Europe. He'd missed the chance to live his dream and backpack across the continent when he finished college.

"It'll be much more fun with you guys. I knew I waited for a reason," he'd said.

Austin and I didn't care where he took us. We were just glad to be out of school for the rest of the year.

We alternated between camping out when the weather was agreeable and staying in nice hotels, especially when we were in cities like Florence and Berlin and Barcelona.

By the time we made it to Scotland, spring was fading into summer, and Dad wanted to sleep under the stars in the Great Glen, the glacial fissure that tore Scotland a new one 400 million years ago. The words *lush* and *green* are all you need to know to describe the Great Glen. Nature done did it right when she painted this scenery.

Smack in the middle of the glen was a series of lochs, one of them being my current home and setting of my nightmare – Loch Ness.

"We can't go to Scotland without spending some time at Loch Ness," my father had said. "Maybe we'll even see the monster!"

We thought that made this place the coolest stop on our trek across Europe.

Kids are stupid.

It was dark. Austin and I were roasting marshmallows over the remains of our fire. Our parents went down to the water's edge to clean out the pot we used for cooking chili. I was playing Shania Twain on the boom box, but had to keep it low. When Austin tried to hit the Stop button, I whacked him on the back of his hand with the hot end of my marshmallow stick.

"Jeez, that hurts you asshole!" he shrieked, cradling his hand to his chest.

"You're such a baby. I can't believe you came out first. Mom saved the best for last."

He chucked a marshmallow at my head.

"You're more like my afterbirth."

I shrugged it off. We'd been saying the same things to each other for so long, we could recite each other's lines.

That was as close to 'twin speak' as we've ever come. We look nothing alike, we act nothing alike, and we sure as hell don't think alike.

It was then we heard the screams.

Two screams, to be exact.

My mother and my father.

We bolted to our feet, spilling the plastic bag of marshmallows into the fire.

There was a tremendous splash of water.

We ran to them, heedless of what we might encounter. Someone was attacking them. A deaf person could hear their struggle, the pain and terror in their cries.

We got to the shore a moment before we lost them forever.

Their heads were visible, floating atop the churning water. Something big and black and shiny, like the body of an anaconda, was wrapped around their necks. It must have given a sudden, powerful squeeze, because their voices were cut sharply.

"We have to help them!" Austin blurted, going so far as to get in the water up to his ankles.

But I held him back.

I watched my parent's eyeballs puff up and explode from their sockets seconds before they were dragged down into the Loch's murky depths.

And just like that, they were gone.

I watch them die every single night.

I can't un-see their eyes, blowing up to cartoonish proportions before popping like balloons filled with mayonnaise and blood.

It's why I fucking hate looking at people's eyes. I can barely stand to look at my own in the mirror. I haven't worn makeup in years just to save myself the horror.

The clock says 4:15.

I'm not the least bit tired.

Early to rise it is.

Maybe today's the day.

If it isn't, oh well. I've got nowhere else to go.

CHAPTER TWO

"Hello, Mrs. Carr."

"Someone's up at the wee morning hours. You must be the only young person I know that doesn't sleep until the crack of noon. I've just put some tea on the kettle."

I plop the basket of groceries on the old butcher-block counter.

"No tea for me, thanks. I'm more of a coffee kinda girl. And I'm not exactly a teenager."

"You're close enough."

Mrs. Carr is the owner of the little shop where I get my food and used paperback books. She's as old as the Highlands and blind as a mole. She's also sweeter than rock candy and the least nosy person in all of Scotland. She's a very rare breed indeed.

"Thirty is a pretty long way from sixteen," I say.

"You're just a baby."

She has to bring each item to the tip of her nose to see the price sticker. The surprisingly new cash register beeps and chirps as she taps out the rolling amount without needing to look down. I trust she's getting it all right.

There's a little community board tacked on the wall by the entrance. I notice that lately there have been a lot of flyers posted about missing dogs and cats. The latest is a pug named Maggie. I'm not a pug fan. Their faces look as if they've been smashed in with a cast-iron skillet. I have to admit, though, that Maggie is pretty cute.

It makes me sad, because I'm pretty sure no one will ever see Maggie again.

Mrs. Carr says, "It's going to be a beautiful day. A nice one to be out on the water, if you can. You know, you can ask Billy Firth about renting his boat. He's always looking to make a quick buck and if you tell him I sent you, I bet he'll throw in some extra petrol for free."

She never remembers that I own my own boat. Score another check mark in the pro column for Mrs. Carr.

"That sounds like a good idea."

I always say that.

I don't know who Billy Firth is and she never volunteers more information – like how I would go about finding him and his magical boat for hire.

"You take care of yourself now, dear. See you tomorrow?"

"You will."

I'm about to step outside when she calls out to me.

"I almost forgot. I just got a box of books and found this for you."

She hands me a yellowed paperback of Michael Crichton's *Sphere*. Somehow, she remembers I like to read thrillers. Crichton books, even ones like this that I've read a couple of times, are like gold.

"No charge. You just enjoy it."

"Thank you, Mrs. Carr. You're the best."

She smiles, the wrinkles in her face smoothing out enough to make her look a few years younger than Noah.

"You tell that to Mr. Carr. Sometimes that old codger needs a reminder."

The little bell chimes when the door opens. The paperback sits atop my bag of fruit, bread and cheese. It smells like someone's attic, which is most likely where it's been moldering since the late eighties.

The sun is melting away last night's clouds, birdsong in the air. There's even a butterfly sitting on the hood of my car, a VW Bug I christened Eileen when I bought her a few years ago. She's sunflower yellow and isn't too fond of the terrain in winter or rainy springs. But I always wanted a Bug, damn the practicality.

The drive up A82 to my RV on the western edge of Loch Ness only takes a few minutes. I remember when going up A82 seemed so picturesque, the wide swath of the Loch peeking out ominously from behind clumps of trees in bloom. Now, it's just the place that connects my living space from where I get my food.

I'm getting very practical in my old age. Or maybe I'm just losing touch with my romantic side. I really would like to meet a nice guy who can sweep me off my feet. It sucks sleeping alone. I've yet to find the man that doesn't head for the hills after experiencing my night terrors all close and personal.

That doesn't mean I won't keep trying. It's just hard to find guys when you live in an RV in the woods. Pubs are fine for quick hookups, but I'm getting to the point where I need more.

At least I will once I get done what I'm here to do.

My RV sits in a small plot well off the beaten path. You can't see it from the main road. The dirt track that winds down to my home is packed tight, thanks to Eileen's treads. If you're on the Loch during the fall or winter when the trees shed their leaves, you can catch a glimpse of my long, tan rolling home. I was told by the realtor that the plot was supposed to be the site of a pair of lake homes, but the investors ran out of money right after the land was cleared.

Score one for me. I came to Scotland wanting seclusion and I got it in spades.

I stow my food in the mini-fridge and contemplate sitting in my folding chair outside and reading *Sphere* for a while. It's still early and there's a nice, soft breeze. It's not like I have a job to go to. I'm not at the mercy of a clock.

But I am at the mercy of something much more demanding.

Sighing, I toss the book on my unmade bed. It'll be there when I get back. I need to burn some of the fever out of my brain first.

Locking up the RV, I saunter down to the boat slip. It was made to hold two boats, but I don't like neighbors. So, I bought up the property next to mine. The money Austin and I got from the insurance company was more than we could spend in our lifetimes.

Accidental death by drowning paid big bucks.

No one believes what we saw.

We were young and traumatized, unable to fully process our parents drowning before our eyes.

Whatever.

My aunt raised us until we were eighteen. That's when the money shifted into our accounts and my brother and I went off to separate colleges, never to return to my aunt's house in Westport, Connecticut. She was nice and all, but a little snooty for my taste. Nothing looks better than Westport in your rearview mirror.

Plus, I think she had been plotting ways to get that money away from Austin and me.

My boat is a twenty-six-foot dual pontoon boat I named Vindicta. It's Latin for revenge.

I didn't name my RV. I just call it home.

Vindicta can hold up to a dozen people. It was designed as a fishing boat, which in a way, I'm kind of holding to that.

It has a sun deck that I use on slow days, just sitting there, soaking up rays but never taking my eyes off the water. I had the motor retrofitted so she's faster than any pontoon boat around and gives a nice, stable ride. She can hold a lot of gear that I stow under the leather couches and lounge chairs. That's most important.

I take her out to the center of Loch Ness. There are a few smaller boats out, men holding on to fishing poles, probably already dipping into the beer.

They don't appreciate the throaty rumble of my boat. Some have so much as told me, peppering in a few colorful words. I try to steer clear of them. I'm not in the mood for squabbling.

It's easy for them to blame me for the terrible fishing this season. They're just not biting. It must be the American chippie in the loud boat.

It's gotten to the point where some university is sending a professor and a few grad students to study the water itself. It's not like we're seeing fish bodies floating everywhere. They suspect some kind of fungus or bacteria, something that's driving the fish away.

Just where to, no one is saying.

I have my own suspicions. Maggie the pug, Bruce the mastiff, Sheena the tabby, and all those unnamed fish are in the same place – a big belly deep under the Loch.

It's hard to not feel anxious.

Not after that TV crew from the US came over to take more sonar readings of the Loch. Someone from town had pointed them in my direction. I was, after all, the crazy American camping alongside the Loch, searching for proof of Nessie.

Word getting out about my, uh, obsession, was all my fault. Chalk it up to way too much alcohol in a pub or two over the years. I'm the loose lips that sink ships.

I'll give the gang from the production crew credit. Even though I refused to be interviewed or have pictures or video taken, they still let me tag along. The producer, a decent-looking, middle-aged guy with a shockingly red beard, wanted to get in my pants. The dork in charge of getting permissions and interviews hoped that by befriending me, they'd wear me down and get me to agree to be part of their dog and pony show.

Both were sorely disappointed.

Though a quick tumble with Red Beard was tempting.

Some strange hits popped up on their third day. Something big was moving under their ship.

Then there was another large shape. And another.

It rattled some cages. Everyone on the boat held their breath, the tension tighter than a Kardashian butt lift. The shapes glided past quickly, disappearing like phantoms.

Then came the cheers. Red Beard served champagne that night. He had proof of the Loch Ness Monster.

Not any kind of proof you could use in a court of law. But in the court of cable-watching America, it was more than enough.

"I hope, at least, we were able to bring you some closure," he said to me that night, his words slurring slightly.

"It ain't over till the fat lady sings," I replied, getting up and heading back to my RV.

I didn't need proof.

I knew the monster existed.

It ate my damn parents.

But Nessie, or better yet, *Nessies*, had laid low for a long while.

Were they back?

If they were, I was going to throw them a welcome home party.

Immediately followed by a memorial service.

CHAPTER THREE

The knock on my RV door startled me. I was so engrossed in *Sphere* that I had forgotten where I was for a moment.

"Who is it?"

The blinds over the little galley table were open. I saw a blue van parked outside.

"Samson Butchers."

Oh, right. I'd forgotten about my little delivery.

I opened the door to a man who looked like a miniature Popeye. He was bald and squinty, with forearms as big as my thighs.

"Afternoon. Are you Ms. McQueen?"

"The one and only."

"Great. Sign here. And where would you like us to put it? You have a cold box somewhere close?"

"You can leave it right there," I say, pointing to the red picnic table.

"On the table?"

"Yep." I scribble my signature on the receipt and hand the clipboard back to him.

"It's awful heavy. You sure you don't want my partner and I to bring it to it's…ah, final destination?"

"The table is just fine. Thank you."

He looks at me as if I've gone off my nut. That might not be far from the truth.

With an exaggerated sigh, he turns back to the van and barks, "She wants it on the table!"

His partner, a kid with a mop of classic Justin Bieber hair, pops out from behind one of the open rear doors.

"You sure?" he says, looking over at me, the fragile woman who clearly doesn't understand what's involved here.

"I'm not, but she is," Popeye says, jerking his thumb in my direction.

I enjoy watching the two of them wrestle the cow carcass out of the van. They bury the meat hooks deep, grunting and puffing with each step. The kid almost pops a vein in his temple when they drag it onto the table with a heavy thump.

"You shouldn't leave it out for long," Popeye says. "It'll spoil right quick in this heat."

"I've got immediate plans for it. No worries."

I step out of the RV to inspect my delivery of prime, uncut beef. Samson Butchers is a wholesale butcher over in Kincraig. You can order your meat online, which is proof that there's nothing you can't do on the Internet.

"Well, good luck to ya," Popeye says, walking stiffly back to his van. Bieber Hair gives a quick wave, rubbing his shoulder.

The slab of meat takes up the entire table. Already there are flies buzzing around. The overhang of trees is keeping the sun off it for now, but it won't come the afternoon.

Good. I have work for Mr. Sun to do.

Three warm days later and you can't see the meat under the twitching black mass of flies. The stench is what woke me up this morning.

I think it's ready.

Tossing last night's sweaty clothes in the hamper, I quickly dress, down a bottle of water along with some supplement pills, jam handfuls of off brand cereal in my pie hole and head outside.

Phew!

It reeks. The buzzing of the flies sounds like something out of one of those devil possession movies. *Oh shit, this is the part where the lady gets possessed! You can hear that demon coming!*

I'm not ashamed to dry heave.

I should have skipped the cereal.

"All righty, Clarabelle, your timer has popped. Time to get you the hell away from my open windows."

Dragging out the rolled-up plastic mat from under the RV, I unfold it beside the table. I also grab a pair of hammers from my toolbox. Swinging as hard as I can, I sink the claw ends into the ripe carcass. This causes a cloud of flies to bolt from the body and encircle my head. They get in my nose and mouth, crawl around my eyes. I can't swat them away because I have to hold onto the hammers.

Spitting a disturbingly large fly from my mouth, I place my foot on the edge of the table and pull with all my might.

Clarabelle barely moves.

The flies, thankfully, leave me to go back to their feast.

They've done some impressive work on the exposed flesh. Just thinking of all the maggot eggs that must be gestating under the surface makes me gag. I pull the collar of my shirt over my nose and mouth and try again.

Every muscle in my arms and back stretches to their limit.

But Clarabelle is moving!

Come on, you dead bitch, I scream in my head, afraid to open my mouth and let the flies waltz on in.

Digging my heels in the dirt, I feel the carcass start to tip over the end of the table. I cry out with something that sounds close to labor pains, making one last tug.

Clarabelle tumbles off the table and onto the plastic mat, taking me with it because I'm too dumb to let the hammers go.

My body drapes over the rotting cow. I feel the crush of dozens of fly bodies against my chest and stomach. My face makes unwelcome contact with the whole mess.

And that's it for me.

This time, my heaves aren't dry, adding to the wonderful mess. More food for the pests.

I stagger to my feet, wipe my mouth with the back of my hand, and run to the water.

I do not pass go. I do not collect two hundred dollars.

I dive into the cold water, clothes and sneakers and all. It's shocking as hell, but I wouldn't have lasted another second with all of that gunk on me.

Going totally under a couple of times, I pull myself onto the dock, exposed to the warming sun. I'm breathing so hard, I think I might pass out.

"Why didn't I just have them put it on the dock?"

Because that would have looked even stranger. They can't know what you're up to, that's why.

It takes me twenty minutes to dry off and settle down enough to tackle the second part of the day's festivities.

This part goes easier.

Since it's a downward slope to the slip, the mat acts like a sled, carrying Clarabelle to the shore. The damn flies will not stop. I'm going to hear their insane buzzing for the next week.

Lifting up one of the seats on Vindicta, I pull out the commercial strength line with the hook already tied off on one end. The hook is big enough to catch a whale shark. Again, another gift from the Internet.

I drive the hook into the carcass, tying the other end to Vindicta. It takes the slightest bump in the throttle to drag Clarabelle fully into the water. The flies storm off, pissed that I sunk their breakfast, lunch, and dinner.

Consulting the map I drew where the TV crew got those sonar hits, I head east into the Loch.

I'll bet Nessie's never had a delivery like this before. I'm going out where you can't get a good curry in under thirty minutes.

CHAPTER FOUR

I stocked Vindicta with enough food and water to last me all day. PB&J sandwiches on brown bread (what we call wheat bread on the other side of the pond) and a bag of apples to keep my energy up. God knows I needed it. The struggle with the cow took more out of me than I thought it would.

Some may say I'm guilty of overestimating myself.

But I always manage to get shit done. It's just not always pretty.

The day passes agonizingly slow. I forgot to bring my book or even a trashy magazine. The boat has a radio, which I keep on low just to hear another human voice.

Slathering on sunscreen, I sit on the end of the boat with my feet in the water.

I wonder how many fish have been nibbling on Clarabelle. I check my own sonar, a Garmin Chartplotter Sounder, one of the best on the market, for the thousandth time.

Just a few little fast moving blips. Nothing spectacular or noteworthy.

Not that I expect anything to happen. Daytime sightings of what the world calls the Loch Ness Monster are rare. If the lake beast, or beasts – since there has to be more than one for it to have survived this long – pop up and break the surface, it's typically at sunset or full night.

I could have waited until then, but I get impatient. Plus, I know the stink of that carcass isn't going anywhere anytime soon.

That picnic table is toast. I've little desire to be anywhere near there right now.

A Loch Ness tour boat glides past in the later afternoon. It's full of foreigners – some taking in the beauty of the Loch, others hoping to catch a glimpse of the infamous monster.

Nessie has been a hell of a boon for the local tourist trade.

Even when the famous 'surgeon's photo' of the creature, it's long neck sticking out of the water, equine head in shadows, was proven to be a fake, it didn't make a dent in the crowds coming to sneak a peek at the most famous waterway in Scotland, if not the world.

I wave to them, proud of their dedication to the truth, even if most of them think it's all stuff and nonsense.

Stuff and nonsense.

I *have* been in the UK too long.

Night finally arrives and my senses, dulled by the long day, perk up.

The pleasure and fishing boats of the day have gone home. It's just me now. I start the engine, keeping Vindicta at a slow pace, trolling the area where I saw those shapes on the sonar.

Now, I know Nessie isn't predictable. If the creatures were, we would have captured one long ago.

But for the first time since I got here, I know they're near.

Call it women's intuition.

That and a solid sonar hit is enough for me.

And the fact that all living things on land and sea are being swallowed into the ether.

"Here kitty, kitty, kitty," I call out. "Come and get your din-din."

My sonar shows the uneven terrain of the Loch's floor several hundred feet below me. At its deepest, Loch Ness is over eight hundred feet. That's a lot of room to hide.

But I suspect they have other places to disappear into.

"That's some prime beef down there. I made sure it was nice and stinky so you can't miss it."

The moon sliced across the still water, sweeping over Vindicta. The temperature was falling fast. Damn, I forgot to bring a jacket.

All the time in the world to plot and plan and I still forget stuff. Maybe this is why Austin did so well in college, and I clocked in three semesters at Jacksonville University before being respectfully asked to leave.

But I have street smarts.

Just not lake smarts. At least not all the time.

It bothers me that I can't remember what my parent's voices sounded like. I have pictures to refresh the memory of their faces, but they weren't big on making home movies.

Those fucking things took that from me.

I know in the Bible it says to love your neighbor, but I'm pretty sure Jesus was referring to people, not lake monsters. Getting all Captain Ahab on Nessie is something even the big guy should understand. I know people think I've lost my mind, or that I'm just a spoiled rich orphan hiding out in Scotland, wasting my life away.

A ripple of waves lap against the pontoons. I teeter a bit, gripping the wheel to keep on my pegs.

I cut the engine.

It's so quiet out here.

Sometimes, when there's low cloud cover, the sounds of people talking near the shore can be heard way out on the Loch. It's kinda eerie, like overhearing spirits conspiring with one another.

But not as eerie as this total silence.

It used to bother me, but I'm used to it by now.

In fact, I prefer the quiet.

I let Vindicta drift in the stillness. I sit back, careful not to make a sound. I don't want to do anything to break the calm. I close my eyes, picturing Clarabelle below my feet, lazily spinning round and round, shredded flesh dancing in the water.

An hour turns to two, then three, and so on. I check my watch every fifteen minutes or so. I'm so tempted to turn the engine back on because I've veered way off course, but then it hits me.

What the hell course am I talking about?

Anywhere on the Loch is the course.

Just sit still and chill.

I dated a guy who was a cop for a year. He was a lot of fun to be around. The man was a roving party. Everywhere he went, merriment followed. He made sure the booze flowed, his jokes getting more and more off-color as the night wore on, but that only made me laugh harder.

He worked undercover for the Vice Squad for a spell. Did a lot of stakeouts. He told me the hardest thing, especially at night, was keeping not only awake, but alert.

I've done enough Loch vigils to fully grasp what he meant.

By midnight, I catch my eyelids drooping. In fact, there's a whole period of missing time. I assume I wasn't abducted by aliens and just nodded off.

"Fuck it."

I hope there'll be enough of Clarabelle left to try again tomorrow. If not, I'll just order another victim.

Victim is a strong word. The cows are already dead. I'm just trying to make their death a little more noble than being fodder for Shepherd's pie.

The engine blares like a screaming jet. At least that's how it sounds to my ears, lulled by hours of silence.

I give Vindicta some juice, anxious to get to my RV now that I've decided to call it quits. Hopefully, I can catch four uninterrupted hours of sleep before I sweat myself awake.

On the way home, I take a quick glance behind me. The water, looking black as the ace of spades, tears into a V in my boat's wake.

But there's something else there; the ripple of a current coming *toward* me, not fading away.

"What the hell?"

Oh yes, there's definitely something following me, just under the water's surface. It's not a trick of the moonlight or exhaustion.

I slow down a bit.

Whatever is coming doesn't.

In fact, it picks up speed.

I barely have time to brace myself.

I watch in horror as it passes under Vindicta. I'm too dumbstruck to do anything but stare with an open mouth like a dummy.

The boat jerks forward with so much force, I almost flip over the back of my seat.

I'm about to cry out with victory, vindication, and any other v-word I can think of when my worst nightmare happens.

Vindicta is pulled so hard, the bow dips straight under the water. The stern does the opposite, the propeller now roaring because it's in the open air.

It's going to flip the fuck over!

CHAPTER FIVE

There's literally nothing I can do.

Whatever is under Vindicta, and I'm pretty damn sure I know what it is, has Clarabelle firmly in its grasp. I hope the hook is painfully in its mouth, too. Because if I'm going to bite the big one here, I want it to suffer – maybe get an infection that slowly and painfully kills it while the bits of my corpse feed the Loch's remaining indigenous fish.

There's no way I can get to the bow to undue the line connected to the cow carcass. The moment I let go, I'm sliding into the water. Not to mention, the tie line is now under the water and taught as a harp string. My knife, sharp enough to cut through leather, is under my seat. Again, if I try to get it, I tumble overboard.

"I hope you choke on it!" I scream.

The stern rises higher and higher into the air. Vindicta is getting perilously close to a ninety-degree angle.

I hear the snap a split second before the pontoons slam back onto the water.

Just like that, it's over.

There's no retreating wake. No sound, other than Vindicta's engine. I hightail it the hell out of there. Nothing follows me.

Pulling into the slip forty minutes later, I find my flashlight, snap it on and tug on the line. There's no resistance. Clarabelle is gone.

There isn't a single known amphibian in Loch Ness that could rip that carcass clean off the line.

"Holy shit. Holy, holy shit."

I knew they were back. Again, I should have been armed and prepared, but five years of fruitless labor made me complacent.

I look down at my watch. It's almost one am.

I do a quick calculation. That means it's seven at night in Chicago.

Running to the RV, my heart having only sped up since I was almost turned into fish food, I barrel through the door. I scoop up my phone, collapsing onto my bed.

The phone goes to voicemail.

I leave a frantic message. I know I'm probably not making much sense, but he'll get the idea. When I hang up, I can't even remember what the heck I even said.

"You better call me back soon."

Somehow, I fall asleep somewhere around the witching hour, my phone still in my hand.

I wake up in a cold sweat, gasping for air. Something crashes on the floor. I take a quick peek. It's my phone. The glass is cracked right down the middle.

Wonderful.

On the plus side, the sun is out. It's after seven. I'm still tired, but it's too late to go back to sleep.

I'm fully undressed when the phone rings. I scoop it up off the floor and see it's my brother.

"It's about time," I say.

"I just got back from this office party," he replies. He sounds like he's had a few. "I almost decided to wait until I got some sleep."

"Seriously?"

"I said almost. Nat, tell me again, slowly because I'm not used to rum, exactly what happened."

"I will in just a sec."

Even though he's thousands of miles away and can't see me, I feel self-conscious talking to my brother in the nude. I slip on some underwear and a T-shirt and sit cross-legged on my bed.

I lay it all out for him, going as far back as what I saw with the TV crew. I figure he may not remember when we talked about it weeks ago, considering his current skewed mental state. When I get to the part about the boat almost tipping ass over teakettle, he stops me.

"Did you see anything?"

"I was a little busy clinging for my life. It was too far under the water and too dark out to see."

"You sure you didn't just snag that dead cow on something?"

I sigh. "First of all, that part of the Loch is about two hundred feet deep. Ain't nothing down there to snag on. Second, I watched it come right for me. It was freaking crazy!"

He stays silent for a long time.

Then he says, "I keep waiting for you to say you're just messing with me."

"I don't play when it comes to this. I shouldn't have to tell you that."

"I'm sorry. Trust me, I don't doubt you."

"The next big question is, when are you getting here?"

"Nat, it's not that easy. I just got this big project, and they have some new people reporting to me."

I want to reach through the phone and give him the mother of all titty twisters. "I think *this* project trumps your little corporate bullshit."

He chuckles, a big snort cutting his laughter short. "I'm kidding. I can't stand this job. I was thinking of quitting on Friday. I just went out tonight for the free food and booze."

"And I'm sure there were some pretty girls."

"Corn-fed Midwesterners. My favorite."

"Get some sleep, sober up, and buy a one-way plane ticket. Text me the details when you're done so I can make sure I pick you up at the airport."

"I will. I will. I just can't believe it. I really never thought…"

"I know. I kept hope alive for both of us."

He yawns into the phone, which makes me realize I'm still pretty sleepy myself. "I may have a surprise for you when I get there."

"Oh?"

"It's a little 'just in case' something I worked on some time ago. Don't ask me anymore because I won't tell."

"Go to bed, dillweed."

"If I can even sleep after this."

I forgot to tell him to get a flight into Inverness Airport so I don't have to travel all the way to Edinburgh or Glasgow. I wait a while, giving him time to pass out from booze and my crazy news, then text him the best way to get here.

My stomach grumbles and I shuffle to grab a granola bar. I'm two bites in, sitting in the captain's chair of my traveling home, looking at the sun's rays shafting between the canopy, when I feel sleep tugging at me again.

My last thought before I give in is: *take it while you can, because once Austin gets here, you're not sleeping until even George W. can say 'mission accomplished' and mean it.*

CHAPTER SIX

I haven't seen Austin in over a year. The last time he came to Scotland was for two whirlwind days while on his way to Paris to meet a woman he met online. He spent most of that time making fun of my RV. I wasn't unhappy to see him go, but missed him immediately.

When I see him at the airport, I barely recognize him.

He's a heck of a lot broader, the stubbled edges of his hairline creeping back, giving him a wicked widow's peak. His swollen muscles ripple beneath his tight-fitting shirt. He doesn't resemble my dopey older brother. He looks, well, like a bodybuilder with a chip on his shoulder.

But he can't change his smile. He drops his bag and crushes me to his chest with one arm.

"Look at you, 'roid boy," I say.

"I've been preparing."

"For what? A part on the new *Jersey Shore*?"

"Hey, while you've been doing your thing, I've been doing mine. Just because I haven't been here doesn't mean I'm not down with our plan." His bag is almost as long as he is and looks heavy as hell. He easily slings it over his shoulder. No wheeled luggage for Mr. Universe.

"You are aware that when we do find those things, you're not going to be wrestling them, right?" I say, guiding him to the parking lot. It's a particularly warm, cloudless day. Heat waves rise from the baking blacktop.

"You don't know that," he says, laughing.

24

I hate flying. Airports, naturally, remind me of being on a plane. It's part of the reason why once I landed in Scotland, I've stayed put. It would have been easy to go back to the States when winter set in. I vowed the next time I'd get on one of those vile flying tubes, it would be to go home for good.

I'm happy to leave the airport. Just being there gives me anxiety.

The Bug is a tight fit for my oversized bro and his bag. He can't help but spill into my side of the car.

"This should be fun," he says.

"At least the drive from Inverness will be quicker than if I'd let you land in Glasgow. I'd have had to cut the roof off of Eileen for a trip that long. You could ride like Dino on the Flintstones."

"Can I make one tiny request?" His hand is out the window, riding the wind current.

"No, I can't get a bigger car."

"I want to make one stop."

"You should have gone back at the airport."

"Ha. No, I want to see the Loch Ness Visitor Center in Drumnadrochit."

I glance at him with exasperation. "Now why on Earth do you want to go there?"

He gives a sly smile. "I promised my lady friend I'd bring her back a souvenir."

"You want to go souvenir shopping?"

"Yeah. I figure it's better to get it out of the way now. Later, we'll have other things to do."

"I should tell you no."

"Ah, but you won't. You're so happy to see me, if I asked you to stand on your head and sing show tunes in the town square, you'd do it."

"I haven't missed you that much, Austin. No one could miss you that much."

He put his hand over his heart. "You hurt me with words, sis. Right in the aorta."

I pass by a trio of cars moving so slow, I'm tempted to flip them the bird, even when I see they're driven by old ladies who can barely peek over the dash.

"You better be careful of that ticker, what with all the stress the juice must be putting on it."

I kid around, but I'm seriously concerned that Austin is augmenting his physique pharmaceutically. How else could he get so damn huge in so little time?

He flexes his pecs. I'm disgusted.

"Hate to break it to you, but this is all natural. You're not the only one with compulsion issues. Once I got bitten by the bug, I haven't been able to stop. By the way, you have any gyms by you?"

I laugh. "You can bench press the boat."

It's early afternoon when we roll into Drumnadrochit. The Visitor Center is jammed with cars and people milling about. As we mingle among them, I feel homesick. I haven't heard this many American accents in ages.

"I think I'll stay out here," I say, leaning against a rail.

He tugs on my arm. "Oh no you don't." I'm dragged along like a rag doll.

The interior is exactly what I pictured it to be – chock full of Nessie paraphernalia, books on the ghosts and castles of Scotland, a looping film on the Loch Ness Monster, and general stupidity.

I want to scream at them, *"Nessie isn't a goddamn cute curiosity! She is a they, and they are killers, plain and simple!"*

Austin stops to watch the dumb movie, then buys a ceramic Nessie figurine, leather wristband, earrings, and a couple of books.

As we head back out to the car, he says, "You know, we should buy the place out."

I stop and stare at him as if his face inexplicably slid off his skull. "And why the hell would we do that?"

"Strictly business." He has to curl into a ball to get into the car. The interior feels like the inside of a pizza oven. I quickly start the car and power the windows down. "After we kill those bitches, this stuff is going to be worth some serious dough."

This time around, he doesn't make fun of my RV. He stows his gear in my room at the rear and sits on the galley bench by the window.

"Now, I don't want you to take this the wrong way, but your place has, shall I say, a malodorous hint to it."

I look out the window at my stained picnic table. Somehow, I'd actually gotten used to the smell Clarabelle left behind. It makes me worry about myself.

"There's the culprit," I say, pointing at the table. "You want to earn your keep, help me dispose of it." I explain how the damn thing got that way.

Austin does all of the lifting. Who needs a gym?

"Where do you want it?"

"I guess down by the boat slip for now. Anywhere but right outside my RV."

Resting the tabletop on the crown of his head, he carries it down to the water, tossing it in with a splash.

"Hey, I didn't saw to throw it in the Loch!"

"A good soak is all it needs. You got anything to tie it to the slip so it doesn't float away?"

I find some rope on Vindicta and he secures the table.

"It'll be good as new in a couple of days."

"Or it'll just stink like the Loch."

"Anything is better than what's coming off it now."

After that, I go back to the RV, grab a six-pack of Black Isle Blonde lager, and we sit on the deck of Vindicta to bullshit and catch up. It's actually really pretty out today. Too bad I can't fully enjoy it.

"I ordered some more meat," I say, sucking down the dregs of my second beer.

"It seemed to work."

"Seemed? Dude, it worked perfectly."

"So we just go fishing until we find them?"

"Find them all, if we're lucky."

He downs his third beer in one huge gulp, letting out a belch that echoes over the Loch.

"This is why everyone hates Americans."

"Burping is like pooping. Everyone does it. Even Europeans."

It feels nice to have him here. I'm nervous and excited about what's to come next. Having Austin by my side gives me more comfort than I'll ever let on to him.

"What's for dinner?" he asks. "And do you have more beer?"

"I was going to barbecue some steaks. I can throw on a couple of baked potatoes. And yes, there's another sixer in the fridge. I prepared it myself."

He pats my shoulder as he passes by.

"Mom and Dad are with us now, too. You know?"

I swallow the lump that bobs in my throat.

"I know. I feel them every day. They've never left this place. I hope we can help them move on."

I hope we can all move on.

CHAPTER SEVEN

This time, I let Austin answer the door when Popeye and Bieber Hair deliver cow number two. My brother grabs one of the hooks and hauls it out of the van himself. Since the table is now in the water, I laid a tarp on the ground. Austin eventually drops it on the tarp, but not after giving the carcass a few deadlifts, the veins on his neck bulging like milk snakes.

"You want a job?" Popeye says, staring at Austin in disbelief.

"I don't think you could afford me," he replies with a crack of his knuckles that sound as if he's breaking them into tiny little pieces.

The delivery men get back in their van. I wave to them. "See you soon."

"They must wonder what the hell you're doing with all of this meat," Austin says. "You don't look like a raging carnosaur."

"I'm sure they do, but I made sure they're from several towns over. I don't think any gossip will come this far."

"Unless they stop at a local pub for a pint on the way back."

Shit. I hadn't thought of that.

"Well, hopefully this will all be done soon and it won't matter. Does King Kong need any help getting our bait to the boat?"

He stares at the white, red, and blue-fleshed meat at our feet. "I thought you said you got the other one all stinky."

My stomach rumbles. I can't believe the sight of raw meat is making me hungry. Add it to the growing list of things I need to talk to a shrink about.

"I did. This time, I want to see if we can skip the ripening process. If this works, that means we don't have to wait a couple of days for things to get nasty and most importantly, we don't have to smell it."

"Good plan."

He bends down, grabs an edge of the tarp, and starts to drag it down to the water.

"Hey," I call out. "I thought you said you had a surprise for me."

He only smiles.

"It's coming. Tomorrow. Be patient."

I take Vindicta out before dusk. Austin keeps taking pictures of the surrounding glen with his phone.

"First souvenir shopping, now you're taking pictures like a tourist. Did you hit your head with a dumbbell or something?"

He stuffs the phone back into his pocket, I think intentionally flexing his bicep while he does it. Must be a force of habit. Move. Flex. Look for swooning chicks and envious dudes.

"I'm doing all of this based on the assumption that this is our last time in Loch Ness. I may want to look back at it someday in my dotage."

"Your what?"

"Old age. You really should have finished college."

"They barely let me start. I'm quite happy with my decision."

The Vindicta sways back and forth. An early evening breeze has been kicking up. The Loch is pretty choppy, especially as we go further out. The slap of the water against the metal pontoons is hypnotic.

For old time's sake, I turn on Shania Twain, keeping the sound low. Austin shakes his head. "You still like that fake country crap?"

"Nothing fake about Shania. She lived in the middle of nowhere and ate moose. That's country."

"Let me ask you a question. Have you heard of any recent sightings? I know you're not big on being neighborly, but I also noticed that you buy all of the papers."

I say, "Not to mention trolling social media, message boards, and every online group devoted to the Loch Ness Monster. Nope, it's been quiet. I think they're getting smarter. They're keeping their ugly heads low."

"I doubt they're that bright. They're frigging fish."

"I'm not so sure, on either count. But I know with their size, they have to eat. And they've been doing a damn good job with the low hanging fruit." I tell him about the fish and domestic pets. "Supplies are dwindling. So we have to entice them to come to us."

"So, we're like a floating food truck."

"If we're lucky."

"It's kinda strange, how our lives turned out, isn't it?" He takes a swig from a bottle of murky water. I wonder if he slipped some protein powder in it.

"Did you know there are some guys who have been camped out on the Loch for decades? They spend day after day with their eyes glued to binoculars and telescopes, waiting to see a hump or ripple. And if they do, then what? Everyone already thinks they're loons. No one would believe them anyway."

He laughs until he snorts. "Isn't that what you've been doing?"

"I've been on the water, my eyes glued to my sonar, waiting for those sons of bitches to return. Whether they make their way to and from the Atlantic or are hiding in the underwater caves that haven't been discovered is anyone's guess. But they do hide away for long stretches of time. I suspect they come back here to feed, a kind of genetic programming. Thanks to weird changes in the weather, I think their food sources aren't what they used to be. Which means we have to get them now, while they're still hungry but still foraging. Pretty soon, they'll just slink back to wherever they call home." I take the bottle from Austin and take a sip. It tastes awful.

I cut the engine just as the orange sun dips below the distant hillside. It makes the tips of the trees look like they're on fire.

"I just want to sit here for a while, let the world below pass the word around that an all you can eat buffet has arrived."

Austin fiddles with the pneumatic spear gun I bought the same week I picked up Vindicta. I may not have been able to use it for what it was purchased for – yet– but I do shoot it off every now and then to make sure it's still in working order.

I have a .44 in my windbreaker pocket.

If those creatures come to feast tonight, we have a couple of big surprises for them. I also have a Bowie knife strapped to my thigh, in case I need to cut the bait loose in a hurry. If the boat starts to get dragged under again, I won't hesitate to sever the line.

Austin aims the spear gun at the water. "If these things are so smart, maybe they won't fall for the floating side of beef ploy again."

"Even in higher life forms like yourself, hunger has a way of trumping common sense."

I realize we're talking real low, just above a whisper. It reminds me of when we were kids and used to camp out in the backyard, telling each other ghost stories. The trick was to see which one would cave-in first and go back inside for the night. Our parents always left the sliding back door open because they knew we'd never last.

In the end, we scared each other silly. It was a draw when it came to who headed for the safety of their room.

Austin says, "Well, that and sex."

"I'm not hooking myself out to these things, but there's nothing stopping you from offering your services."

He does that little dance thing with his pecs again.

"Please, stop doing that. It's revolting."

"I don't think Nessie could handle me."

I cover my mouth when I laugh so I don't wake up the whole Loch.

And then it hits me – why Austin has turned himself into Schwarzenegger.

Our dad was a scientist, a nerd, a bookworm. He was slightly shorter than our mother and thin as a table leg. I once saw him struggle to carry a cooler of drinks to a picnic my mother laid out in a park in Madrid.

When he and Mom were attacked, there was no way he could fight it off.

Austin was just making sure if the time came, he'd succeed where our father failed. To protect not just himself, but me as well.

I rise from my seat and give him a quick hug. He stiffens.

"What's that for?"

"Can't a sister hug a brother?"

"When they're both carrying weapons and waiting for a lake monster to appear, it's kinda strange."

"Well, we are kinda –"

Something takes a quick, hard hit at the body beneath Vindicta. We both stumble forward, falling to our knees. The tip of the spear is inches from my face.

"Do not touch that trigger," I warn him.

He sweeps the gun away from me and I take a good, deep breath.

Austin runs over to the sonar. "I don't see anything."

"It probably got a chunk and sped off. Here, I'll keep an eye on the sonar. It's better if you have that spear ready."

This time, I'm better prepared. I use a belt to fasten myself to the captain's chair. I stare at the sonar, but there's nothing to see. Austin takes a knee by the bow, spear gun at the ready.

"Any incoming?" he asks.

"Not yet."

Something sweeps past the periphery of the sonar, but it goes too fast for me to tell what it could be. I have to be careful. Every dark shape is not the monster. There are some pretty big fish in the Loch, too. Just not any that people are able to snag on their hooks lately.

It gets so quiet, the drumming of my blood pulsing in my veins is overwhelming.

And there it is.

"We've got something coming up straight for us."

"Where?"

"Starboard."

Austin changes position, the spear gun aimed at the water.

"Holding steady," I say, captivated by the huge, dark shadow emerging from the depths. Where we are is a little over four hundred feet deep. Whatever this thing is, it swept into view at the very bottom of the Loch and is making a beeline for our bait.

"I can't see a damn thing," Austin complains. "It's too fucking dark. The water is like ink."

"I don't want to turn on the lights and scare it off."

"Yeah, but I have a eunuch's chance in a whorehouse to hit this fucker."

I reach for my .44.

"You will if it gets close to the surface."

"And if it doesn't?"

The thing was a hundred feet away and approaching fast.

"It's almost here."

Austin lifts up one of the lounge cushions and finds a pair of goggles.

"Still at starboard?" he asks.

I'm puzzled, too wound up by what I'm seeing on the sonar to comprehend what the heck he's doing.

"Yeah…it's still…why are you putting those on?"

He kicks off his sneakers and drops his shorts to the deck.

"I'm increasing my odds."

And before I can say another word, he hops over the side of the boat and into the water.

CHAPTER EIGHT

"Austin, no!" I scream. I no longer care about keeping in stealth mode. I flip on the bank of overhead lights, including the handheld spotlight. Struggling to undo the belt around my waist, I stare in horror at the sonar as the massive shape blocks everything out.

"Get the hell out of the water!"

Vindicta is hit so hard, she's lifted a foot off the water. The pontoons smash back with a tremendous splash.

I get the belt loose, but I'm immediately pushed back into the seat.

The creature has the bait, and it's taking off with it.

Unfortunately, it's taking Vindicta and me along for the ride.

"Austin."

My heart drops into my stomach. I'm speeding away from him, somewhere under the water. If he's still alive, he's out there, totally exposed.

How am I going to find him if I can break free?

Vindicta is motoring like a speedboat, and the engine isn't even on. The creature is faster than I'd ever expected, especially considering it's tugging a boat along.

I have to cut the bait free.

Dropping to my hands and knees is the best way to keep some equilibrium. I crawl to the bow where the line is tied. I withdraw my knife, putting the handle in my teeth.

We're heading for the northern end of the Loch, further and further from my brother.

I make it to the line, which is literally singing from the tension. I have to be careful. If I don't cut it close, any slack will whip right back at me and possibly take out an eye.

The knife is the width of my palm and can split hairs. I take one quick swipe right by the metal loop attached to the bow, sending up sparks.

Vindicta instantly slows down.

I watch the departing wake of the creature, cursing it.

As it crosses into a bridge of moonlight reflecting on the onyx waves, I see a black hump emerge for just a second before slipping back under.

And then it's gone.

Shit. I have to find Austin.

I scramble back and gun the engine to life. Turning Vindicta in a tight circle, I eyeball my way back to where he jumped overboard. I estimate we've gone at least five hundred yards.

I have to be careful. I don't want to accidentally run my brother over, either. Even though the night is chilly, I'm dripping with nightmare sweats. My teeth chatter until it hurts. It's hard to keep control of my hands. I'm so balled up with adrenaline and fear, I doubt I can spell my last name.

"Austin! Austin! Can you hear me?"

I throttle the engine back as I get to where I think he should be.

Please, please, please be all right.

I scan the water with the handheld spotlight.

My stomach cinches when I think, *if there's one, there could be others.*

"Just shut up," I say through gritted teeth. My jaw hurts from trying to keep them from clacking like mad.

My breath catches in my throat when I spot a lump in the water. I train the spotlight directly on it.

"Austin?"

It looks like a head.

Oh dear God.

It's not moving.

I steer Vindicta closer, slowly, despite my desire to just jump right in.

It is a head. Part of his back is also showing.

"No, no, no, no."

I hop over the bench so I can reach down and grab him. It's hard to see through the tears.

My hands flutter as I attempt to get hold of the collar of his shirt. He's so heavy, I don't know how I'll get him back on board.

I can't stop sobbing.

Pulling with everything I have, his dead weight suddenly disappears.

"Miss me?"

Austin spins out of my grasp, grinning while treading water.

I fall back onto my ass.

"What?"

He lifts the spear gun, minus the spear, and hands it to me.

"I had the right idea," he says. "I'm pretty sure I nailed it."

"Did you...did you just decide to play dead to fuck with me?" I'm wiping back my tears, hoping he can't see them in the dark. I want to hug him first, then kick him in the balls.

He pulls himself back onto the deck. The Loch runs off him like a waterfall. "It was a last second thing. Before I saw you coming back for me, I'll admit I was pretty freaked out."

I punch him square in the chest. He chuckles. I nurse a sore fist.

"It really took you for a ride," he says. "Freaking crazy."

"I thought you were dead."

He slicks the water off his head with his palm. "I told you, Nessie can't handle me. But damn, it was big. I couldn't see much, but it made for a pretty good target. I think I got it right smack in the center of its body. At least it looked like the center."

I shakily get back to the captain's chair and head back toward home.

"Promise me you'll never do that again," I say.

"What? Shoot the damn thing?"

"You know what I mean. Being reckless won't help us at all. That's not the way to honor Mom and Dad."

I see that hits home. The macho mountain of a man instantly looks like a scolded, repentant boy.

Good.

"You're right. I got carried away. But I didn't want to miss my chance."

"That was just one creature, and one chance. We have a shitload of work to do and I need you in one piece to do it."

We ride back to the boat slip in silence. I know he's humming as much as I am.

Despite his act of stupidity, it worked again. These things are hungry as hell and reckless.

Now I know what to do tomorrow.

And somewhere out there, if Austin is right, there's a wounded Loch Ness Monster. I wonder if the wound is enough to kill it. And if the body floats to the surface, who will be the lucky one to find it and make the discovery of the 21st century?

CHAPTER NINE

We slept like the dead that night.

I didn't even have my nightmare.

Probably because I'd lived one hour before. There's just so much a girl – or guy – can take.

I got up before Austin, who was sawing redwoods. His arm had fallen over the side of my makeshift couch and his hand was on the floor. I just missed stepping on his fingers as I crept past him to slip outside with my laptop.

It was an overcast day, with rain to come in the afternoon. This had been one of the driest springs in the Highlands in decades. No one was going to complain about a little rain. In fact, I'm pretty sure some of the locals were doing rain dances in their yards. Gardens were yielding brittle weeds and lawns were as brown as paper bags. This is not the way things are supposed to look in merry old Scotland.

I went to the Samson Butchers' site and placed yet another order.

"You're gonna need a bigger van," I say, smirking at the screen.

The Nessies like beef.

Well, I'll give them as much as they can handle.

The confirmation page says it will take two days to deliver my order.

I click over to the weather channel website and look at the five-day forecast.

Rain and more rain.

Even better.

I want the Loch all to myself. The rain will keep a lot of people away. But those damn tour boats never stop. Too much money to be made.

A bridge to burn when I get to it.

Today is also the day for Austin's surprise. For the life of me, I can't figure out what he has in store. Lord knows, he gave me enough of a surprise last night when he jumped overboard like he was in some 80s action movie.

Oh, and playing dead.

Ass munch.

I brew some coffee, which wakes Austin from his coma, sit in a lawn chair, and wait for the rain.

And my big surprise.

"Yeah. Yeah. No. Umm, yeah. Everything? Good. See you soon."

Austin disconnects the call and sits opposite me. We're at my kitchen table, which is also my dining room table, work desk, and the best place to rest my beer.

"That sounded like a stunning conversation."

He sits so far back in the seat, the wood cracks. He jumps up, apologizing. "Please don't destroy the furniture, you big ape!"

"I don't know how you do it. I almost got wedged in the shower before."

"That's because I'm not as wide as the shower. And neither were you last time you popped by."

He makes a muscle, kissing his biceps. "Don't hate the dedication to perfection."

"Are you sure you're Austin McQueen? He's a kinda nerdy guy, a little unfocused."

He points a sausage finger at me. "Hey, respect your big bro."

I'm about to respond with a witty rejoinder when the sound of a car honking draws my attention.

As I've said, my RV is out where the buses don't stop. No one comes by unless it's for a delivery. I look outside. The rain is picking up, gray skies making it difficult to see the Loch beyond the trees.

And that's when I see a pink minivan pull up. There's a rainbow painted on the side door. Swaying fuzzy dice hang off the rearview mirror.

"Who the hell is that?" I say.

Austin makes me jump by grabbing me from behind and yelling, "Surprise!"

"You bought me a minivan from the gay pride parade?"

The minivan's engine idles, smoke curling from the exhaust. I can't make out who's behind the wheel. Whoever it is, they're not in a hurry to step out into the sheets of rain.

"Even better."

He opens the RV door and waves.

There's a quick honk in reply. Then a man steps out; square-shouldered, short blonde hair, thin as flagpole. He strides over to my brother and they shake hands, neither seeming to care that they're getting soaked.

"Nat, I'd like you to meet my good buddy Henrik Kooper, with a K."

I step aside so they can get inside. Henrik offers me his hand. His grip is strong. I feel callouses on his palms, indicating he's not as frail as he looks.

"Hello, Natalie. You can call me Henry," he says with a slight German accent.

He and Austin drip-dry on the carpet.

I look over at Austin. He just stands there beaming at Henrik.

I say, "Soooo, my brother has kind of hinted to me that you're my big surprise. Do you strip or do a singing telegram or something?"

The tall German catches my gaze, following it all the way to his less than masculine minivan.

"Oh, that," he says. "Camouflage."

For what, I think, *hiding out in the land of My Pretty Ponies*?

"I think I'm going to need a little more."

Austin breaks out of his trance. "Dude, take a seat. You want a beer?"

"I'd like that, yes," Henrik says. "You have any light beer?"

Austin looks to me. I shake my head. What's the point of beer if it has the potency of water?

"That's fine. I'll just drink half."

We sit around my table sucking on bottles of Bass ale. I'm anxious to hear what the hell this is all about. "What the hell is this all about?" I ask.

Austin motions for Henrik to take the stage.

"I can understand your confusion. I know how this must look, especially now that I get the feeling your dear brother neglected to tell you anything."

"He has a habit of doing that."

He takes a pull from the long neck. "Well, your brother and I met at a convention in Cologne almost two years ago."

"That's when I was working for that publisher," Austin interjects.

Henrik nods. "I worked for a German publisher at the time. They specialized in non-fiction books about preparedness."

"Preparedness?" I say. "Preparedness for what?"

"Oh, just about anything – nuclear holocaust, military coup, widespread power loss, pandemics. They published a great many books, with translations in over twenty languages. Uncertain times make people anxious. And when they get anxious, they tend to look further than the tip of their nose."

I rub my temple. "Okay, so you guys are at a book convention."

Henrik smiles warmly. He looks like the world's most compassionate doctor. I can easily picture him in a white, oversized lab coat, a stethoscope draped around his neck.

"Yes, well, as you can imagine, there's more play than work at these events. One night, over one too many cosmopolitans, Austin tells me what happened to your parents."

"He did what?"

I rise from my seat, glowering at my brother. We swore we would never tell anyone the truth after we'd been utterly dismissed by the police and our own family. Why the hell would he tell a total stranger at a book convention?

"Calm down, Nat. It's okay," Austin says.

"Your secret is safe with me. It *has* been safe with me. You see, he only told me once he found out that I wasn't just an editor. I'm well versed in most of the books I've worked on. I've been a, how do you Americans call it, a prepper all my life. I'm especially adept when it comes to weaponry."

I sit down only because Henrik and Austin look so sincere. I can see they're concerned about the sense of betrayal I'm feeling at the moment.

"He wants to help us," Austin says.

"Help us? With what?"

I finish my beer in one savage swallow.

Henrik flashes that smile again.

"To avenge your parents. You do want to kill what people call the Loch Ness Monster, do you not?

CHAPTER TEN

So, the cat's not only out of the bag, it's running around the RV like its tail is on fire.

Hearing Henrik say it out loud almost makes it sound absurd. Almost.

I start, "Look, Henrik –"

"Please, Henry."

He's so calm, it's unbalancing my agitation.

"Henry, I don't know who you really are. I have no idea what your motivations are. You'll have to forgive me if I don't get up and do a happy dance that my brother has made our lifelong pursuit a threesome."

Austin winces. "Please don't say the word threesome when you refer to me. You'll ruin the whole concept."

I ignore him.

Henrik…Henry and I are in a bit of a stare down.

I decide I like Henrik better.

He's looking back at me with crystal blue eyes filled with something that looks irritatingly close to pity.

He reaches across the table to touch my hand, but I pull back.

"I know exactly what you've gone through," he says in a voice soft as melted butter.

I get up and turn my back to the both of them, starting out the front windshield of the RV. The rain hammers it with steady pelts.

"I lost my father in a similar way when I was just five years old," Henrik says.

I look over at him. There isn't a hint of sarcasm on his face. Even Austin looks unusually subdued.

"What? How is that even possible?"

"Your brother and I found each other for a reason. You see, my father was a big game hunter. He made a living as a tour guide for other hunters, taking them on specially charted expeditions all around the world. He took my mother and me along with him on a trip to Indonesia. You have to understand, that was a very rare occurrence. These were hunting junkets. Very macho stuff. They were no place for a woman and child. But he'd been there many times before and was in love with the country. He was going to show us all the unusual sights once the hunting expedition was over. Unfortunately, he didn't live long enough to do so."

"I'm sorry to hear that," I say, wondering how a guy dying in a hunting accident was anything like watching your parents murdered by a lake monster.

Henrik pauses, staring at his beer bottle.

Austin nudges him with an elbow. "Tell her the rest, bud."

When he looks up, I see the faint shimmer of tears in Henrik's eyes. The pain is still very much there, even though it must have been thirty or more years since he lost his father.

I fully understand not being able to overcome the grief, to just let go.

"My father took us deep into the interior. We camped in a clearing that was said to be in proximity to the lost city of Gadang Ur. Now, there was no way to confirm this, as the ancient city is still quite lost, but my father had gathered enough information from the locals to feel we were close. The reasons for going to that location were twofold: there was the possibility of making a great discovery, and any place that had been hidden from human eyes for millennia would be rife with worthy game.

"I remember being frightened by the darkness and absolute silence. It felt as if we were in a place where man wasn't meant to be. For a boy who lived in the city, it felt alien. One night, there was a disturbance in our camp, which immediately put us on alert on account of the preternatural quiet of the surrounding jungle. It sounded like a stampede. But there were voices as well. Not in any language we could discern. My father grabbed his rifle and burst from our tent. I slipped from my mother's grasp and followed him. I was both scared and painfully curious."

I sit back down. I can't help it. I'm drawn in. I've never been so quick to empathize with another person before.

"Have you ever heard of the Orang Pendek?" Henrik asks.

I shake my head. "No, but I have heard of the Montauk Monster and the Dover Demon. Is it like them?"

Austin chimes in. "It's the Indonesian equivalent to Bigfoot. Only they're not as big."

Henrik's face screws up tight. "But they are strong...and vicious. There were three of them that night, savagely tearing the camp to pieces. My father managed to shoot at one before they swarmed over him. I...I could only stand there and watch them literally tear him apart, limb from limb. I'll never forget his screams. A sound like that should never come from a human being. His murder seemed to drain them of their bestial fervor. They ran before my mother got hold of me, carrying the pieces of my father with them. We never found them."

I don't think I've taken a breath.

I want to say, *"Your father was drawn and quartered by Indonesian Bigfoots?"* But that would sound rude as hell. I know what it's taking him to tell me his story. I can see the trust in his eyes. In me, he sees one of the few people on this Earth whose knee-jerk reaction won't be to tell him he's full of crap.

Even if I hadn't lived through my own personal hell with a mythical creature, I think I'd still believe him.

Austin breaks the silence. "I promised Henrik that when the time came, if he helped us, we would help him."

I nervously tap the wet side of my beer bottle.

"So, you want to kill these Orang Pendeks?"

Now there's a fire in Henrik's gaze. "I *will* kill them all. But I've always known I can't do it alone. Nor can you with your pursuit. I think you'll agree that my assistance in your quest will prove to be invaluable."

Austin gets up, the back of his head banging off one of my cabinets. He doesn't seem to notice he just about brained himself. I think we're all numb just about now.

"Henrik has something he needs to show you, Nat. Let's get wet!"

We leave the warm, dry comfort of my cramped RV and step into a shower on full blast. My bra is soaked through in three steps. Henrik pushes a button on his key fob and the side door of the minivan slides open.

"Unfortunately, we need to stand outside. I can't show you if we're all in the van."

"Why's that?" I say.

"I need to be able to lift up the floor."

Austin stands close behind me while Henrik's fingers run along a seam on the carpeted floor of the minivan.

"Ah," he says.

There's a click, and the second row of seats moves to the back of the minivan on a pair of metal rails. Once they're tucked away, the floor rises, like a trapdoor in a haunted mansion.

"Your Loch Ness Monster has never seen the likes of this," Henrik says.

Holy Christ on the cross!

Within the bowels of the girly minivan rests an arsenal that would make Rambo weep.

There are handguns and rifles, something that looks like a grenade launcher, an open box of grenades, and a row of what appears to be small propane tanks.

"Planning on doing a lot of barbecuing while you're here?" I ask him, pointing at the tanks.

"Depth charges," he replies. It's hard to hear him over the pounding rain. "They'll disorient the beasts as much as they will dismantle them. I'm confident they've never encountered anything like it before. The element of surprise, and sheer brute force, are what you're going to need to eradicate these waters for good."

"Where did you get all this?"

"I was in the KSK, Germany's Special Forces Command. I may have retired, but one never loses their special connections."

I can't believe what I'm seeing. There's enough in the minivan to go to war.

Which I guess we are.

"I wasn't going to let you try to take them down with spear guns and a Dirty Harry special," Austin says, placing his wet arm over my shoulder.

I don't need to ask if any of this stuff is legal.

I do wonder how we'll be able to set off all of these explosives without drawing the unwanted attention of the entire region. But for now, I'm going to assume that my brother and Henrik have thought of this, too.

"I don't know what to say," I say, taking it all in.

"I'm hoping when we're done here, you'll say, 'When should we meet in Indonesia?'" Henrik says with a slight smile.

At this moment, I can't say no. Flying across the globe to settle the score with a band of Orang Pendeks (I'll have to Google them later) seems reasonable, considering what Henrik has brought to my door.

I catch his eye and reply, "Okay. You're in the gang. Shaggy here can show you where to bunk tonight."

Austin laughs. "Zoinks."

CHAPTER ELEVEN

With Henrik now on the team, the RV feels smaller. I'm not used to waiting to go to my own bathroom. Or the special smells guys leave behind. My bedroom is a foot and a half from the bathroom, so there's no escaping it.

The rain is still coming down, but for now, not so much that I expect to see an old man in a robe outside leading pairs of animals away.

Austin and Henrik are awake and dressed in matching black tracksuits.

"Going for a run?" I ask, rubbing some crust from the corners of my eyes with my knuckle.

Henrik tosses a bag at me. I watch it bounce off my chest and fall to the floor.

"Good reflexes," Austin says.

"I just woke the hell up."

"So sorry," Henrik apologizes. "I brought a suit for you, too. Austin gave me your size estimate. I think it will fit."

I pick up the bag. It's clear plastic, with a neatly folded, vacuum-packed black track suit inside. "Just because we're in this together does not mean we're going to be dressing alike."

Henrik frowns. "No, no, no, this is not a fashion statement. It's a matter of comfort and practicality. You see, these tracksuits are completely waterproof. They're very lightweight and flexible with airtight zippers."

Austin pulls his zipper up and down rapidly, over and over, working out some tune that I'll never figure out. "I went outside before. The rain just slides right off. And I'm nice and dry underneath."

I curl my lip in disgust. "I prefer not to think about what's going on under your clothes."

"I thought it would come in handy when we go out today," Henrik says.

"Today?" I grab a carton of orange juice and take a gulp. Henrik looks squeamish. I know what he's thinking. *I won't be drinking orange juice or anything from a carton while I'm here.* "My big beef bonanza doesn't get here until tomorrow."

My brother smiles. "That doesn't mean we can't get things started today."

I'm almost afraid to ask.

"Now?"

"Now is always better than later," Henrik says. He's not exactly ordering me to get my ass in gear. He's just enthusiastic, and going by Austin, it's contagious.

Those Germans and their efficiency.

"Okay, give me a few minutes. But I think I'll pass on the waterproof mafia costume."

Henrik shrugs his shoulders. "I understand. Consider it a gift, thanking you for allowing me into your sacred circle."

Sacred circle?

I turn my back on the boys. Better enjoy the bathroom while it's empty and free of bad odors.

The carpeted deck of Vindicta squishes under our feet. It's a flat deck, so water just runs over the sides. The Loch is pissy today, the chop rocking my boat enough to make walking difficult.

Austin and Henrik have the hoods of their tracksuits up. The only things wet on them, according to my roided out brother, are their faces.

"This is so cool," Austin says. "I could stay out here all day."

I, on the other hand, am soaked to the bone. It feels like there's a swimming pool in my socks. I have to tie my hair back to keep the wet strands from smacking me in the face.

"What's in the bag, Dad?" I ask Henrik as we pull away from the slip.

He pats the side of a silver briefcase.

"This is something very special. All will be revealed soon."

All righty.

"Anywhere in particular you want to go?" I ask over the sudden gust of wind that's brought a lashing sweep of rain with it.

"I was thinking of somewhere in the vicinity of Urquhart Castle," Henrik replies.

"Urquhart Castle? That's miles away," I say.

The crumbling castle is probably the most famous landmark on Loch Ness. The old, picturesque ruin squats on the northwestern shore. I read that it was built in the 13th century, standing for four hundred years until it was finally left to rot around the 17th century. Only sections of the façade remain. It also happens to be one of the favored spots to set up camp and search for the Loch Ness Monster. I guess history and monsters make good bedfellows.

"We have plenty of time," Austin says. "Did you have other plans for today?"

I want to come back with something biting and sarcastic, but he's right. My only plan today was to sit down and finish *Sphere*, maybe take a nap. I thought it would be best to marshal my strength for the days to come.

I turn the wheel and give Vindicta some gas. "Urquhart Castle it is."

It takes a while to get there, the storm swelling and ebbing. There's no real overhead protection on a pontoon boat, save a retractable canvas cover I can put up that covers a small portion of the boat. I'm wetter than a mermaid, secretly regretting I didn't wear the tracksuit.

You can normally spot the castle from a pretty good distance, but visibility is in the sub-suck range today. I spy what looks like the outline in the distance.

"We're here...I think."

I cut the engine and Vindicta sways with the motion of the Loch.

The hazy, ruined ramparts of Urquhart Castle loom ahead of us. It sits on a wide spit of land like a lone sentry. I guess this is why so many people have come here to look not just for Nessie, but to absorb the full beauty of Loch Ness and the surrounding glen. Without the rain and fog, it's really quite beautiful.

Today, it just looks ominous. The water of the Loch looks black as oil. Anything can be down there. I try not to let my imagination run wild.

"Then it's time for this," Henrik says, unlocking the clasps on the mysterious briefcase. When he opens it, I see a black box nestled in a foam cutout. He pries it out and attaches a wire to a connector on top of the box. The spool of wire ends in what appears to be a little buoy.

"What does that toy do?" Austin asks. He has to raise his voice to be heard over the pounding rain. Water drips off the tip of his nose.

"Hopefully, it gets the beasts hungry."

That little box doesn't look all that appetizing.

"I hate to tell you, but these things don't eat cast offs from Radio Shack," I say, hands on my hips, daydreaming about dry clothes.

Henrik fiddles with a couple of dials on the face of the box. There's a loud burst of sound that makes Austin and I jump. It sounds like a wounded duck.

The unnerving sound seems to satisfy Henrik. He then carefully lowers it into the water. He unspools the wire. I estimate it must be ten or fifteen feet long. The buoy bobs on the Loch's surface.

"What was that sound?" Austin asks. We're all watching the little buoy like expectant fathers.

"That was the distress cry of a Merganser duck," Henrik says, beaming with pride.

"A Merganser duck?" Austin says.

"Yes."

I would be just as confused as my brother if I hadn't been living here for the past five years.

"You know those black ducks we see everywhere?" I say to him.

A light goes on in his head. "Oh, that's what those things are called. I thought a duck was just a duck."

I joke, "If it quacks like a duck…"

Henrik says, "As I'm sure you both know, Merganser ducks have been mistaken innumerable times for the monster. Because of their black heads and necks, when they swim on the water, especially when it's dark, they can be mistaken for the rising head of the creature – at least by overzealous or overly imaginative Nessie enthusiasts. I'm also sure that they provide a valuable food source for whatever lives down there. To a predator, nothing sounds more appetizing than wounded prey."

A look of concern washes over Austin's face. "That's all well and good, Henrik. But what if it works? We didn't bring any of the big guns on board!"

It's funny how my twin brother has taken to calling him Henrik now. Shows who wears the pants in the family. Or jeans, for the most part.

He's also right. I even left my .44 behind. The only thing I have onboard is a spear gun, and that's not going to do much.

"All we need is contained in the device."

I have to keep Vindicta moving so the buoy doesn't float out of our sights.

"I have one more question," I say. "Why did we have to come all the way out here?"

When Henrik sits down, water squishes from the seat's cushion with a loud squelch. "I know how popular this location is…for people. Which means it would be quite *un*popular for the creatures. If we can lure them here, to a place I'm betting they avoid, it proves the efficacy of the device."

Austin squints against a gust of rain that slaps him full in the face. He says, "Where on Earth did you get a recording of a hurt Merganser duck?"

Henrik's face sours and he breaks our gaze. "It's homemade. It's not something I'd like to talk about."

I shoot Austin a look. Up until now, I've liked Henrik. He's been polite, intelligent, honest and the bearer of an incredible arsenal. And if I'm being honest with myself, a tad attractive. I'm not usually into slim, neat guys, but I'm also in no position lately to be picky.

But he also tortured a duck.

I don't know how to process this little tidbit of information.

I don't have time, because Austin shouts, "Look. The buoy just took off!"

It sure did. The little thing scampers away from our port side, moving at a decent clip. It could be a fish has it. There are some big salmon around. But would a salmon have a hankering for duck?

"Follow it, Nat!" Austin says, moving to the front of the boat.

"Really? I wasn't sure what to do."

I keep the buoy as close as I feel comfortable. I'm grateful it's not attached to the boat. At least we won't be upended this time.

Henrik takes something else out of the briefcase. It's as small as a car key fob. He holds it between his thumb and index finger.

"Almost," he says.

"Almost what?" Austin says.

The buoy is moving faster now. Whatever has it wants to beat feet.

It dips under the water and is gone.

"Shite," I exclaim, allowing for a little of the local color to bleed into my frustration.

"Perfect," Henrik says. He presses a red button on the fob. I expect to hear the little beep beep of a car door opening. He counts down on his fingers. "Five, four, three, two, one. Stop the boat!"

I throttle back and put the engine in neutral.

"What's going on?" I say.

"That wasn't just a playback machine. It was also a very powerful electrical charger. I just activated the charge. If one of your lake monsters has it in their mouth, it should momentarily incapacitate it."

Austin and Henrik scan the water. I can barely see around them.

"You just electrocuted a Loch Ness Monster?" Austin says, clearly impressed by the technology.

So far, all I know that it can really do is play back the sound of a poor duck that Henrik bludgeoned. I'm not as impressed.

"We shall see," Henrik says.

"Or not," I add. I've been here a long time. It's made me a bit of a pessimist.

We wait for what seems an eternity, me trying to keep Vindicta in the same general area, fighting the current, fighting the wind, fighting the damn rain.

"I see it!" Austin points ahead.

Even though it's the afternoon, I click my handheld spotlight on to get a better look.

I can't believe what I'm seeing.

CHAPTER TWELVE

Bubbles rise and pop at the surface. It's not quite like the moment before Godzilla rises from the deep – it lacks the visual drama – but I find myself holding my breath.

"Now we see the results of the shock," Henrik says. "It was either too little, just enough, or too much. I'll take the two latter over the former."

"We want it to be juuuust right," I joke, but it's a nervous quip.

"Goldilocks of the Loch," Austin says, though I can tell he's just as tense as I am.

For a brief moment, the weather gods smile on us and the rain slows to a drizzle.

And then we see it.

The shape just breaks the top of the turbulent water. It's long, maybe twelve feet or more, but I can't make out any specific details. The waves do their damnedest to push it back under.

"Nat, get us closer," Austin says. He's grabbing for the gaffer pole.

"You're not pulling that aboard if it's still alive," I say. If that thing wakes up and starts thrashing around, we're fucked. I don't enjoy the idea of trying to swim home from here. If it doesn't eat us first.

He levels the pole toward me. There's a sizeable steel hook on the end.

"Trust me, I'll make sure it's dead," he says.

"We could tether it to the side of the boat," Henrik adds. "When we get back, we'll have time to study it, really get to know what we're up against."

Austin stands at the ready with the steel rod. He looks like an Olympic pole-vaulter, ready for his shot at the gold. I'm still not too keen on getting this close without any assurance that it's departed from the land of the living. Henrik dips into the briefcase and takes out a taser.

He catches my eye, shrugs, and says, "Just in case."

It better hold one hell of a charge, because the thing in the water is huge. I'll bet it eats dolphins as snacks.

I pull Vindicta right up alongside the creature. I run to the side of the boat. I have to see it clearly for myself.

The neck is long and bent downward. The head is somewhere under the dark water. Its body rounds out, looking like a long manatee. The back end tapers off, becoming more snake-like. I can see a powerful back flipper. The body rolls a bit, and the front flipper comes into view.

I gasp, and I'm not much of a gasper.

"Do you see that?" I say.

"That's a surprise," Henrik says.

The front flipper ends with what look to be five fat fingers, with webbing between the digits. Each finger is tipped with a curved claw. This thing could tear the face off a person with one easy swipe.

"Kill the fucking thing," I tell Austin. "Go right for the neck."

It's big and it's dangerous and I know odds are, it isn't the exact beast that killed my parents. But I didn't come here to play the pan flute for these things and connect with them on a spiritual level.

Austin raises the pole. "You know, we can make a fortune off this if we want to sell pictures and the rights to our story."

"I'm sure people will line up to hear the heartwarming story of the two Americans and one German arms specialist who set out to kill Scotland's favorite pet."

He pauses to consider my point, then says, "You're probably right. It's not like we need the money anyway."

No, we don't. We're here to eradicate these creatures and hopefully get out of Dodge with no one the wiser. Even if these things never show up in Loch Ness again, the tourists won't stop coming. Commerce always trumps reality.

"Here goes!"

Austin plunges the sharp end of the pole at the creature's neck.

The hook glances off its oily flesh. Austin loses his balance. The pole slips from his hand and goes into the water. Henrik and I rush forward to keep him from following it.

"What the hell is that thing made of?" Austin bleats, searching overboard for the pole. It's probably twenty feet under and sinking fast.

"You did scratch it," Henrik says, pointing out a jagged red line on the neck.

"It must be pure muscle," I say. "At least you and it have something in common." Austin doesn't appreciate my humor. I think he's upset that his manliness was just thwarted by a sleeping giant.

Henrik leans so far over the rail, I worry he'll fall. "That confirms it." He straightens up and turns to us. "It's not dead."

"How do you know?" I ask.

"Because unless my eyes are playing tricks on me, it's still breathing. But the good news is it's out cold. It didn't even flinch when Austin stabbed it."

"It might not feel that if it was awake," Austin says. "That neck is solid as granite."

So now we have a slumbering lake monster and only a handheld taser to protect ourselves when it wakes up. I'm not liking where this is going.

"You guys can forget tying it to the boat," I say. "For all we know, it could be wake up any minute. I don't want to be attached to it when it does."

Henrik nods rapidly. "No, you're very right about that. Maybe it's best we put some distance between us and it. We can watch it revive with a safe buffer between us."

I don't need to be told twice. Austin looks like he wants a second crack at it, but I'm all out of gaffer poles.

No sooner does Vindicta's engine let out a rumble of retreat than the beast thrashes, throwing up white plumes of foam. We pulled about fifteen yards from the thing, which is about one yard clear from bearing the brunt of its spasms.

Water splashes over the pontoons, drenching the deck. I make like a tree and leave as fast as Vindicta will go. The creature looks pretty angry.

It couldn't spend at least a few groggy minutes before Hulking out?

"I think we've seen and learned all we need today," Henrik says in his calm, neutral tone. He can't take his eyes off the clearly unhappy lake monster.

"Understatement of the century," I reply.

Something breaks the surface on the other side of the boat.

I see a hump a second before it descends. The V of a great underwater wake points straight toward the restless beast.

"I think the cavalry is coming," Austin says. His knuckles are white as a fish belly from gripping the top rail.

Vindicta kicks into high gear. I'm so glad I had its motor overhauled. A regular pontoon boat would still be churning away in the danger zone.

The hump becomes visible again, this time right next to the monster we zapped. Its frenzy immediately stops. In an instant, both disappear. It's as if they were never there.

"Holy shit that was close," Austin says, breathing pretty hard. There's a smile of relief and astonishment on his face. I'm pretty sure I'm wearing a matching one.

"Unreal. It makes you wonder how people haven't had encounters like that before, what with everyone trolling around here for decades."

Henrik sits back on one of the lounge seats. "Because no one has ever come here with the intention and equipment to harm them before. We can consider today quite the success."

I'm so jazzed, my fingers shake on the boat's controls.

My brain won't stop buzzing, thoughts churning in a dizzying whirl. Did the wounded one send out a distress signal that brought the other to its aid, or did they travel in schools like fish, or packs, like wolves? Those eerily human fingers on the flipper haunt me. It's almost like they're the prehistoric link between amphibian and the eventual transformation to man when they pulled themselves onto dry land. I know it's impossible, but I can't shake the thought from my head.

"We're going to a pub, any pub, and the drinks are on me," Austin says.

I'm about to second that emotion when something smashes into the port pontoon. Vindicta dangerously tilts for a split second before settling back to stasis.

I bite my lip and taste blood. I look down at the gauges. We're going as fast as we can.

A slew of curses flow from my mouth like chocolate at a fondue fountain. "Those mothers are chasing us."

I look back and see several humps cresting the rain-dappled water before submerging again, presumably to get under Vindicta and flip her over, leaving us floating around like fish food. I shout choice words at Henrik and his damned gadget. He can't hear me through the wail of the boat.

Wham!

Wham!

The pontoons on each side of the boat are dinged, one after the other. I lose my grip on the wheel for a moment. Austin and Henrik are hunkered down. There's nothing any of us can do except pray that Vindicta can somehow outrun these bastards.

Or bitches. I don't want to be sexist about the matter.

I have her pointed to the shore, mentally calculating the depth of the water. If we can last long enough, sooner or later, the lake monsters are going to run into shallow water, at which point I pray they're intelligent enough to turn tail rather than beach themselves.

I have a strong feeling they're not dumb animals.

Austin keeps looking back at me, his face white as death. Henrik is transfixed by the rising and falling humps.

There are no other boats around. We're the only witnesses to what I'm sure is the first case of a boat being chased by Loch Ness Monsters. For once, I don't like being first at something.

"They're gone," Henrik shouts.

I turn around. Sure, I can't see any more humps, but that doesn't mean they're not right under us.

Refusing to be optimistic, I keep the engine humming at max power. If it overheats or just plain explodes, we're in deep shit.

"Come on, baby, just a little further."

We make it to a square of a floating dock, the kind kids swim out to and jump off on hot summer days. There's a small ladder on one side. I swing Vindicta around the dock, finally slowing down. It should be way too shallow here for anything that size to safely follow.

No one says a word while we wait.

Rainwater blurs my vision and I have to keep wiping at my eyes.

After fifteen minutes of absolute silence, I finally exhale. "I think old Bandit just left the Smokey in the dust."

Austin lays his head back, letting his face get pummeled by fat raindrops. "That was some good driving, sis. Can we go to the bar now?"

Henrik remains quiet.

I'm soaked and exhausted and in need of many, many drinks.

"We sure can."

Hugging the coastline, we make it to my slip without any further attacks. Austin has to grab my arm to keep me from falling when I get off the boat. My legs turn to mush the second my feet touch dry land. It takes me a few seconds to shake it off.

I keep thinking, how many of those things are out there?

Do they have memories?

Will they know Vindicta the next time we head out?

Worst of all, will they want to do us in as much as we want to make them a memory?

I feel as though we've just lost an advantage.

CHAPTER THIRTEEN

Austin wanted to go to the trendy Nessie's Tavern, but I wasn't having it. After today, I've had my fill of Nessie. Plus, that tourist trap this time of night is always three deep at the bar. I don't need the headache.

Instead, we go to the one tavern I've been known to pop in from time to time, the Thorny Crown. The religious overtone of the name says little about the dark, smoky, seedy interior. The older barflies congregate at the end of the bar, watching some soccer match on the TV. They give us a quick, disapproving look when we walk in, then immediately dismiss our presence. An old Hank Williams song is playing on the jukebox. I was surprised to see how many people in Scotland love good old American country music.

"Charming," Austin says, sidling up to the empty corner of the U-shaped bar. "Nothing like a pub where you can smell every piss ever taken."

"You're free to walk down to Nessie's. It's only about a mile and a half. You can get your quad or lat work in or whatever it is you do."

Sean the bartender is a portly guy in his early sixties. He's got a whopper of a mole right between his eyes. I learned a long time ago not to stare, but my brother is hypnotized.

"I see you found some strays. What'll it be?" Sean says.

"Three whiskeys and three pints, Sean. I'm thinking of adopting these lost souls." I lay my money on the sticky bar.

Sean casts them a sideways glance. "Just make sure they're toilet trained."

He pours the whiskey and stout beer and ambles back down to the regulars.

"To surviving," I say, toasting with the glass of whiskey. We clink glasses. Henrik and Austin knock the whiskey back and wince. I take a nice, long sip, savoring the taste, the burn reminding me that I'm not cooling in some creature's belly.

Henrik looks pensive. He has questions. I can tell. I have plenty of my own, but there's no one around to ask. After today, we may be the world's foremost authorities on Nessie, and that's not saying much.

"So, do you have any more little gadgets like that?"

Henrik sips his beer. "A couple."

"Do me a favor – the next time you bring one aboard my boat, tell me what the fuck it is and what you're planning to do with it. That way, we can plan appropriately."

The pontoons took a beating, but there weren't any breaches we could see when we made land. I hope Vindicta is still above water when we get back.

His cheeks redden. "Please, accept my apologies. I had no idea that would happen."

"No one could have foreseen that," Austin says. I shoot him a *don't give him any excuses look.* "Either of you have a guess as to how many were out there with us?"

I scratch my knee. It's been hours and my legs still feel weak. "I don't know. Three?"

Henrik leans back in his seat. "Five."

"You sound pretty positive." Austin cracks his knuckles, an annoying habit that started right after our family trip that resulted in only half the family making it back to the States.

"I looked for distinguishing marks. I'm not sure you noticed, but each one has certain scars, just like whales or sharks. Living underwater isn't a life of leisure. If my observations are correct, there were five unique creatures out there, including the one we stunned."

I want to ask Sean for a bag of peanuts and crisps, but I don't want him over eavesdropping just yet. "Where there's five, there could be five more."

Austin leans against the bar. "I don't think so. You and I have always known there has to be more than one of these things in order to survive. However, I think their overall numbers have to be low." He holds up his index finger. "First, a gaggle of Nessies would destroy the ecosystem."

I remind him about the current lack of fish in the Loch and the growing concern of the locals.

"Yeah, but that would have happened a long time ago if there were too many big boys down there."

"And girls," I add, tipping my Guinness back and drinking half the glass. "Without them, you don't get more boys."

Austin rolls his eyes. "*And girls.* Consider this – the greater their numbers, the greater their chance for discovery. I mean true discovery, not blurry pictures or shadowy video. It's almost as if nature keeps the family small so they can remain hidden."

Henrik looks to me, his cobalt eyes shimmering from the booze. "You've been here for years, Natalie. What do you think they are?"

I've been waiting for Henrik to ask this question ever since he dragged his soaking butt into my RV. I'm surprised it's taken him this long.

"I'll tell you what they're not. Dinosaurs. I don't buy that whole plesiosaur theory. It's cool and intriguing because if one dinosaur managed to survive here, there have to be others, right? Jurassic Park could be just around the corner, only we round up the dinos rather than grow them in a lab." I finish off the whiskey and motion for Sean to bring another round. "Eels were a popular consideration for a while, and it's one that I keep filed under 'mmm, could be.' Then there's catfish, fresh water sharks, a branch of chimaera fish, seals. You ever been to the zoo or an aquarium?"

Henrik nods. "Of course. Several in different countries."

"You ever see a seal?"

"Yes."

"Then you know how dumb that is. And catfish? What's out there isn't going to end up on some creole dinner buffet."

Sean slides our drinks over. Austin, the big macho man, sucks down the shot and chugs the Guinness. Good to see he's loosening up. "Okay, you're great at telling us what it isn't. I personally fell for the plesiosaur story for a long time."

"And now?" Henrik asks.

"I've moved past that, mostly based on some of the things I said before. Dinosaurs take up a lot of space and need a lot of food. So, Nat, what are you putting your money on?"

It's funny. Austin and I grew real close after our parents were murdered. Even though we've been on different continents, we stay in touch as much as possible. The one thing we rarely discuss is the true nature of the Loch Ness Monster.

I shrug my shoulders and look into the creamy head of my beer. "I have no fucking clue. Whatever they are, they're something we've never seen before. A whole new species. And when I say new, I mean really new. I know that the legend goes all the way back to the sixth century and the account of Saint Columba."

"I read about him," Henrik says. He looks like a kid who just got the right answer in social studies class. "He supposedly saw the creature attacking a man in the water and he used the power of God to drive it away."

Austin shakes his head. "Yeah, he exorcised the Loch. Why didn't we try some 'power of Christ compels you' when we had the chance, Nat?"

"That whole story is a crock of shit. Those old saints did a lot of crazy, impossible stuff if you believe everything you read. When you get right down to it, the Loch Ness Monster doesn't really poke its ugly head out of the water until the 1930s. I'm sure there were plenty of hoaxes that followed, but basically, we're dealing with something that has about an eighty-year history. In terms of world history, that's less than a popcorn fart."

Henrik doesn't get my humor. Or he doesn't eat popcorn. Or fart.

I continue, since the boys are hanging on my every word. "What we have is a brand new species struggling to survive.

Don't ask me how they came about. I'm no biologist. By the time we get to the eighties, the species hits hard times. There's a die-off. That's why sightings are few and far between. But, at least one male Nessie and one female Nessie carry on, and get it on. Maybe they tunnel under the silt in the Loch's bottom to care for their young. Or find some underground cavern to raise a family. Every now and then, they need to venture forth for some food." I think of my parents, the looks on their faces as that monster squeezed the life from them before dragging them down to a watery hell. I feel tears coming on, but will them the hell away. "Well, the kids have outgrown the home, and they're out and about, as we can attest."

Pausing to drink my whiskey and beer, I notice that Sean is giving me the hairy eyeball.

I think he doesn't approve of my companions.

Being the lone American chippie happy to frequent the bar, it was never hard to quickly become the center of attention. The local boys dig my accent as much as I can't fathom theirs. Tonight, all of my attention is on these foreign guys and I guess Sean isn't a big fan of change.

I turn away from Sean and say, "In conclusion, this is our chance to get them all, before whatever wiped most of them out before rears its ugly head again. We know they're around, and hungry and responsive to our bait. Next time we go out there, we go loaded for bear and finish this."

Austin slides off his stool. "Great speech. I gotta take a wicked piss."

Henrik pats my arm. "I liked it very much."

"Gee, thanks."

CHAPTER FOURTEEN

Because I wasn't expecting to have to feed another person, I head over to Mrs. Carr's for some provisions.

My nightmare rocketed me awake at a little after five. I stayed awake, my brain buzzing with all of the things we have to do over the next few days. It's also buzzing a bit from a hangover, but I solve that with two aspirin and enough water to drown a sea turtle.

I give *Sphere* back to Mrs. Carr.

"Did you like it, deary?"

"It was great. Thank you again for thinking of me. Hopefully, you can pass it on to someone else."

I doubt it'll survive another reading. The spine cracked to the point of being soft as tissue and the pages are barely clinging to the dried-up glue.

"Oh, I'm sure I will. Plenty of people about who like a good science fiction story around these parts. It doesn't look like today will be a good one to be on the water. I don't suppose you'll be needing to rent a boat."

I look outside the display window. It's gray and gloomy and raining. It's supposed to be like that for the rest of the week. Perfect.

"Not today, Mrs. Carr. I have other plans to keep me busy."

She gives me a beatific smile. I just want to hug her; she's so adorable.

For someone about to go to battle with a family of monsters that almost killed me, I realize I'm awfully happy. Perhaps I've just gone native and appreciate a dreary day.

The boys are still sleeping it off when I return. The butchers will be here in four hours. The inside of the RV smells like sour booze sweat and farts. Thank God there's a collapsible awning on the side of the RV. I set it up, grab a trashy magazine, and settle under it, listening to the tap-tap-tap of the rain plinking on the canvas awning. I love the smell of rain in the morning. It's so comforting.

"You have a fly in your mouth."

I wake up so startled, I almost fall out of my chair.

Henrik stands over me with a towel draped over his shoulder. "It's gone now."

My magazine must have fallen and blown away while I slept. It's a waterlogged blob in the mud where my picnic table used to be.

"What time is it?"

Henrik checks his watch. "Almost eleven. Here, your awning leaves a little to be desired."

He tosses the towel on my lap. I'm not soaked, but I am damp all over. At least it's not from my terror sweat.

"I was thinking about what you said last night. About the creatures being a new species. I can't help but wonder if we have a responsibility to preserve at least one of them in the interest of science."

Rubbing my face and hair dry, I stare at him from under the towel. "Any chance you brought a big ass cage in that cute little van of yours?"

He looks back at the pink delight.

"Um, no."

"Well, I don't have any plastic bags that'll hold one like it's a goldfish at a county fair, so I guess we're out of luck."

I can see Henrik will not go down that easy. "Perhaps if we wound one so it's complacent enough to be tugged in. We can call a university or even that television network and have them do with the body as they wish."

I hand the towel back to my German co-conspirator.

"It's not like we can stick around and take a bow. We're going to stir things up pretty bad. We'll be lucky to make our exit without getting arrested, much less waiting around for some scientist to claim the find of this or any other century. I'm sorry, Henrik, but we're here for one reason only – to kill those bastards."

"And bitches," he adds.

"Right. And bitches."

"I understand, Natalie. It was just a thought."

"You want to save an Orang Pendek for that *Finding Bigfoot* show when we're in Indonesia?"

"Point well taken. Now, I believe your bait is about to arrive."

We hear the vans rumbling toward us before we see them. My little plot of land is about to get a bizarre makeover – modern outdoor slaughterhouse. It's all the rage in Europe.

"Hey, muscle man! Time to earn your keep." I slap my hand on the side of the RV.

My brother comes out in that black jogging suit. "Afraid of a little rain?"

"What, I like it."

Henrik raises an eyebrow at me. "At least someone appreciates it."

I'm not going to tell him that I plan to wear mine tomorrow.

The cows come home, this time without Popeye and his shaggy haired assistant. My strange order may have wigged them out.

It takes us the better part of twenty minutes to get all dozen carcasses out of the two vans. We lay them on the ground, in the wet leaves and pine needles. These drivers don't ask any questions, especially after they eye the big tip I hand over to the guy with the clipboard. I'm sure they'll talk about us later. The key is, I won't be around to hear it.

Austin is breathing heavy, having done most of the lifting and shifting bodies around. The muscles on his arms are raised like little racecar tracks. It's a tad unsightly. "Now what?"

"We prepare Vindicta for tomorrow. I'll show you guys all the little storage nooks and crannies. She can take on a lot of gear."

Henrik wipes the cow blood on his hands on some leaves. "I have a lot of gear to give."

"And Austin, I elect you to carry those depth charges because they look heavy."

"This is better than the gym."

"I know most gyms are meat markets, but this is going to an extreme," Henrik says, opening up his rainbow van.

I'm happy to see Vindicta is afloat. I keep checking on her, waiting for some fatal crack in a pontoon to appear and literally sink our entire mission. She's one tough bitch.

By the time we're done, Henrik and I are soaked to the marrow, whereas Austin in his now smelly tracksuit can't stop talking about how dry he is. Vindicta sits lower in the loch. Her speed will be compromised. That's a concern. Those things are fast. All my years of planning didn't account for an arsenal provided by a German with the polite nature of a maître de.

With any luck, we won't need to run away. When they come at us, our job will be to face them head on until there's nothing left of them.

Still, it's nice to have the option of living for another day, should things go sideways. And I smell sideways blowing on the wind.

"She looks heavy," Austin says. We stand on the shore, looking at Vindicta. There's nary a weapon of monster destruction in sight.

"I thought you liked girls with a little meat on them."

"I do. But not when I need them to carry my ass around."

Walking back to the RV, I hear my cell phone chirping. Austin is already here, which means it can be one of only a couple of people. I'm not big on giving out my number. Hell, I don't even exist on social media. I'm a total outlier in my generation and I make no apologies.

I run into the RV, tracking in a full cloud of water. "Yeah."

"Nat? It's Rob Rayman."

"Hey, Rob. You keeping dry in that tent of yours?"

"I had to ditch the tent last night. The car is much more waterproof. Listen, I thought you should know about what I just saw. Or what I think I just saw."

"Why don't you come over and tell me in person. My brother is here."

"Do you have coffee?"

"Yep."

"Hazelnut?"

"Don't push it."

"I'll be there in twenty minutes or so."

Austin has unzipped the top of his jogging suit. I catch him admiring his solid chest, pecs bigger than my own tits. "You really are in love with yourself."

"Just checking out the definition all that lifting brought out. Who was on the phone?"

"A guy who's just like me. Lives on the other side of the loch. He's coming over. Please put a shirt on. I don't want him getting all hot and bothered."

Henrik stands on the narrow steps by the door, letting the water drip from his clothes and under the door. "If you want some privacy, I can drive a bit."

"No, I'll want you to hear this. You can make yourself useful and get some coffee started. Make a lot. Rob is a caffeine addict."

CHAPTER FIFTEEN

Rob Rayman quit his job as a school administrator in Ohio ten years ago to devote his life to capturing definitive proof of the Loch Ness Monster. He's short and narrow, with slicked back gray hair and loaded with nervous tics. The locals all think there's something wrong with him, aside from the fact he lives in a tent most of the time, setting up cameras night and day in the hopes of catching a glimpse of the monster. He reminds me of a bird sipping from a birdbath, knowing several cats are close by and watching his every move.

He's one of a half-dozen, full-time monster hunters on Loch Ness. A couple of the others have gotten their fifteen minutes of fame, being featured on specials about the Loch Ness Monster, interviews on the news and newspaper and magazine articles.

Rob, with all of his fluttering machinations and compulsions, has been kept under the radar. People sum him up in one word: kook.

Naturally, Rob is the only one I talk to. He's actually quite bright, a victim of a skittish temperament brought on from a nervous breakdown the year his wife died and he lost his job. It brought out a raging case of OCD, and he's been fighting it ever since.

"Greetings and salutations," he says, scratching at the back of his neck like he's trying to dig something out from deep under the skin.

"Long time no speak." I hand him a steaming cup of coffee. He takes it in both hands.

"Ah, sweet elixir from the gods. So, which one of you is the infamous Austin?"

"Infamous?" Austin pouts. It looks off-putting on that beefed up meatball face.

I make the introductions all around.

"Are you a Nessie enthusiast , too?" he asks Henrik.

"I'm very enthusiastic to assist Natalie and Austin."

It comes to me that I never want to play poker with Henrik. The man knows how to play it cool.

We gather around my less than spacious kitchen/dining room table.

Rob says, "You planning on having a big barbecue?"

I'm not sure where he's going with that one. He sees my confusion, because he quickly adds, "All those sides of beef you have out there. Looks like you're ready to feed all of the Highlands."

"I'll tell you all about it after you tell me what you saw."

"Promise?" Now he's tapping his heel against the floor and tugging at his eyebrow. I know in his head, he's counting.

"Promise." That stops the eyebrow tugging.

He takes a long sip of coffee. "Mind you, it all happened so fast, I didn't catch it on camera. You'll have to take me at my word."

Rob has dozens of cameras around him at all times. I wonder how he could miss anything.

Austin sits so close to me, I'm almost pushed off the bench. Henrik stands beside Rob.

"I saw it early this morning, right around sunrise. Well, if the sun would have been able to make it through this cloud cover. I got out of my car to, ah, relieve myself. I'd had a hard time staying asleep, what with all the racket the rain was making coming down on the roof."

"What did you see?" Austin asks impatiently. I can tell he wants to add, *I bet it's nothing like what we saw.* I pat his forearm, a gesture I hope he interprets as *keep it down, boy.*

Rob blinks his eyes rapidly for a bit, then says, "It was on land."

"You saw the creature on land?" Henrik says, crossing his arms.

"Yes. It was about fifty or so yard away from me, between a stand of trees. I watched it kind of slither around them for a few seconds. I think it realized I was watching, because next thing I knew, it darted right for the loch. It barely made a splash when it hit the water."

Henrik's mouth is open. "And you say it wasn't in the water at first."

"That's what a land sighting implies," I remind him.

"But, it's a lake creature."

Austin gets up to refill Rob's coffee. "Not entirely. In fact, one of the very first sightings of the creature in the 30s happened on a road not far from here. A couple was in their car, driving home one night and they saw this strange animal loping across the road, headed toward the loch."

"That was just the first of many," I add.

Henrik takes a seat. "But that would mean they can breathe air. If that's the case, how can they stay under water for so long?"

"Maybe they can do both," Rob says. "Or, as I've often posited, we're looking at two separate cryptids."

The thought of having to track and take down two types of monsters gives me a headache. I really don't want Rob to be right.

Austin sits back down, shaking his head. "I don't think this area could support and hide two unknown animals. If it did, there would be sightings and close encounters all the time. Logic says they're one and the same."

Henrik stares into his coffee.

"Like the *Creature from the Black Lagoon*."

I break away from watching Rob dab at his lips with a handkerchief to ask, "Come again?"

"Did you know there are three *Creature from the Black Lagoon* movies?"

Austin, who is no movie buff, says, "I'm not even sure I saw all of the first one."

Rob nods excitedly. "Yes. There was *Revenge of the Creature* and then *The Creature Walks Among Us*. The quality degrades with each sequel, but I love them all."

I have to ask. "What does a movie monster have to do with this?"

"They say the inspiration for the Gill Man, as he's affectionately known, came from the discovery of the coelacanth, a fish that had been thought to have gone extinct millions of years ago, until a live one was caught in 1938. You see, the Gill Man in the movie lived underwater, but could also breathe for a time on land. Once it was captured and surgically altered in the last film, it lost its gills and became half-man, half-creature. I wonder if the creators also drew from these reports of a land and lake monster in Scotland. A little art imitating life."

"I'll call Universal and find out." I turn my attention back to Rob. "How long did your sighting last?"

Now his shoulders jerk back four, five, six times. "I'd have to say close to twenty seconds."

"And you didn't get one shot?"

"My cameras, the few I had up that early, were pointed at the loch, and naturally not the spot where it dove back in. It's like those damn things know. I was so overcome, I don't think I moved for a good five minutes after it disappeared. To realize that everyone was wrong and I haven't wasted my life out here, it's a bit overwhelming."

I feel both happy and sorry for Rob. Yes, he now knows he isn't crazy, despite my assuring him of that for years without revealing my own experience. When the dust settles, he's going to beat himself up about not getting it all on film. He's in his mid-sixties. I'm sure he'll worry about whether or not he'll be this side of the dirt if and when he gets his next crack at it.

Looking at Austin, I can see the hamster wheel turning in his own brain.

"Rob, that's just incredible," I say. "See, I told you to stick with it."

"You did, you did. Thank you, Natalie, for never giving up on me."

"Can you excuse us for just a second?"

I pull Austin to my bedroom and close the door.

"I want to let Rob in."

He massages his scalp. "I don't think he'll be much help taking down those things."

I shake him off. "Not that. Poor guy might stroke out if he had to grapple with one of them. No, I want him to film it."

"Oh, and have our faces plastered all over the world as the great monster murderers?"

I look at my made bed, my neatly folded change of pajamas on the pillow. I'm suddenly very tired.

"I'll tell him to make sure he only shows the creatures. He's good for it. This way, he gets all the notoriety. And he'll be able to sleep at night, not toss and turn with thoughts of what he missed."

Austin takes a deep breath, pacing around the room. There's enough space to take about four steps, so it's really mini-pacing.

"If you trust him, I trust him."

"I do."

"Guess he'll be like one of those wartime photographers."

A jolt of concern runs through me. "Yeah. We just have to hope the military doesn't swoop down and take all his stuff away."

"He'll have to make backups of backups and stash them all around before he goes public. I can help him with that."

I give my brother a hug. It's like embracing an anvil. "Thank you. We're going to make that man very happy."

Henrik is listening to Rob retell his story, asking for descriptions of the creature. The coffee has Rob's nerves singing. He's talking like an auctioneer.

"Rob, I have something to tell you."

He cuts his tale short, staring up at me with shining, emerald eyes. This morning's encounter has turned him back to an excited kid.

While he traces the outline of his jaw with his fingers, I clue him in to what we're planning to do. When I'm done, I've never seen him so quiet. He says nothing, all of his tics vanished.

After a long while, he says, "You're going to kill them?"

"Yes. I have a very good reason for that, and I can tell you if you want to hear it."

He shakes his head. "I know you wouldn't do it without some measure of validity. It just seems very extreme."

"An extreme circumstance is what started all of this."

"And you want me to capture it on film so the world can see?"

Austin leans into him. "Yes. You'll be as famous as the Loch Ness Monsters themselves."

"No one will ever doubt you again," I add.

I'm not sure if it's physically possible to smile from ear to ear, but Rob gives a good go at it.

"I'm in."

CHAPTER SIXTEEN

I must have been screaming, because when I wake up in a tangle of soaked sheets, Austin and Henrik are standing over my bed. One of them had turned on a light, and it stings my eyes.

"Oh, hey there."

Austin sits on the bed, rubbing my arm. "Wow, that must have been a good one."

I roll over to grab a fresh towel from the floor. "Oh, aren't they all. I'm sorry I woke you guys up."

Henrik looks uncomfortable. He keeps looking away from me, arms crossed tight across his chest. "Are you all right?"

I look down and notice one of my boobs is slipping out from under my shirt. Austin doesn't see it, thank God! I adjust myself quickly, getting out of bed so I can go to the bathroom and change.

"No, but this is normal for me. Go back to sleep. It never hits twice in the same night."

"Maybe what you're planning to do, when it's finished, will give you peace." Henrik smiles weakly. His eyes are puffy, his normally neat hair askew.

"One can only hope."

I splash water on my face and the back of my neck, change real quick, and pad back into my bedroom. I can see Henrik hunkered under a blanket.

Austin is still in my room. He's lying in the bed, reading something on my tablet. When he sees me, he pats the bed.

"Come on, I'll help you get back to sleep."

"I don't think that'll work anymore."

"You never know until you try."

My brother is no stranger to my night terrors. He suffers from them as well, but nothing as severe as mine. The memory of our parents dying will swell up and knock him for a loop a handful of times a year. He says it's getting less and less with the passage of time.

Me, I'm stuck. Zero progress. Of course, my current living condition indicates I have some ways to go before I move on.

"I can just stay up. It'll be dawn soon, anyway." I get back in bed and lay on my side, facing away from Austin.

"There's no rush. We're not farmers."

I feel a tug at my hair. I know he's twirling the end between his fingers.

"Remember when you buzzed all your hair off?" he says.

"It was the cool thing to do back then."

"No, it wasn't. You looked like a little boy going to summer camp. You only did it to piss people off."

I can't help smiling as I recall the look of abject horror on my aunt's face when I came back from my friend Cindy's house. Cindy's father had a set of professional clippers. Cindy's skills were less than professional, but I didn't look like I had mange.

"Maybe," I murmur.

When we were younger and barely coping with what had happened, I developed a nervous habit Rob Rayman would have envied of twirling my hair so I could fall asleep. Then, one night when I woke up too terrified to close my eyes, Austin lay beside me and twirled my hair for me. Something about the warmth of his presence and the strange comfort of my hair being twirled put me at ease enough to fall back to sleep.

It had been a long time since Austin had been the Natalie whisperer. To my amazement, it was working. My eyelids felt heavy as full-grown Nessies.

He whispered so softly, I couldn't tell if he was speaking or if I was dreaming. "Henrik's right. When this is all finally over, you're going to sleep like a baby every night. Mom and Dad are always with us. And I know they're proud."

I was drifting when I hear something heavy shuffling outside the RV. I open one eye. Austin drops a strand of hair. I feel it fall onto my neck.

There's a deep snort, then the sound of something being dragged through the leaves.

I have enough time to sit up before the RV is rocked so hard, I worry it's going to tip over.

CHAPTER SEVENTEEN

Austin and I slip right off the bed. The RV cants, then settles back with a mini sonic boom, the shocks creaking like hell. It sounds like half my possessions went crashing to the floor.

"Crap, crap, crap!" I run to the front of the RV, passing Henrik who is reaching into his duffel bag for something.

After our earlier conversation with Rob, I should have known better.

"Take this," Henrik says, handing me a gun that's so heavy, I almost drop it.

Austin is right behind me. Henrik gives him a gun as well. I'm very glad we didn't load everything on Vindicta earlier.

The RV has a kind of picture window with a plastic shade. I grab the cord to the shade. "We don't go out there until we see what we're dealing with."

The RV is slammed again and I topple into Henrik.

"You really need to put in a bell so people don't have to knock so hard," Austin says, holding on to the table.

I rip open the shade.

We can't see much at all. It's still night, the rain hasn't stopped and we're surrounded by dense trees.

But we can hear the creature – or creatures – moving about.

"Do you have a light for outside?" Austin asks.

"I did, but it broke."

"Flashlight," Henrik says calmly.

I rush to the console between the two front seats. It's filled with maps and junk. I dig like a frantic dog until I find the little flashlight that's been in there since I bought the RV. I hope the batteries aren't dead.

Pressing the flashlight to the window, I look back at Henrik and Austin. My brother looks like he's either ready to jump out of his skin or beat someone out of theirs. Henrik just looks ready.

"Here goes."

The flashlight clicks and miracle of all miracles, a harsh shaft of light stabs the darkness.

"Holy flipping Christ!"

The creature's vile face is right outside the window. It looks like something from an old-time freak show, an animal inbred to the point of utter deformity, a pickled horror guaranteed to scare the ladies.

If a donkey fucked a flounder, and its baby was forced to sit next to a microwave for a year, you'd get what's staring back at me. Its flesh is gray-black, with brown speckles that look like melanomas. The eyes are bulging black marbles, one drooping much lower than the other. There's one nostril, leaking a custard-like fluid that I just know smells like the devil's armpit. It has a perfectly round parasitic mouth with saw blades for teeth. Before it smashes its ungodly head into my window, I also spy floppy ears, the ends appearing to have been chewed ragged.

The glass spiderwebs but doesn't break.

"Don't shoot through the glass!" As thin and fragile as the barrier is, I don't want it gone entirely.

Henrik is already unlocking the door. "Keep the light on it for us!"

The creature turns away, dashing back to one of the cow carcasses. And that's when I see the other one.

"It's not an it. It's a them," I shout back.

Austin snaps his head around to me. "How many?"

I shine the light all across the field of bait. As far as I can see, it's only the two.

Yeah, *only* two.

They're massive. Their bodies are built like undulating dragons, minus the wings. Their strong talon-tipped flippers propel them with almost the same ease as gliding through the loch.

I hear the RV door open.

Now the darkness is lit by brief flashes of suppressed gunfire. I hadn't noticed that all of Henrik's guns have silencers. I wonder if the Germans have an equivalent of the Boy Scouts. Henrik would have graduated with all of the merit badges and then some. The last thing we need is to wake up every soul in a mile radius.

I don't dare move from the window to join the boys. If I do, they'll lose the light. Even a couple of seconds could be deadly.

The beasts flee from the shots. One of them carries an entire cow in its mouth with the ease of a cat toting around a ball of yarn.

They're exceedingly fast. So fast, they escape the reach of my flashlight in no time.

"Don't go after them!" I shout, but it's too late. Henrik and Austin are right behind them, unloading their clips.

I run into the rain. What if one of those things decides to stand its ground? It'll kill them before they can kill it. Handguns won't be enough.

"Austin! Henrik!"

I'm not sure they can hear me through the rain and the stampede of the fleeing Loch Ness Monsters. I see bursts of light and run toward them.

One of the creatures cries out, a strangled whine that sounds as off and irregular as it looks.

"Got it," I hear Austin cry out.

"Look out," Henrik shouts.

My heart falls out of my mouth. My eyes blink in response to the flare of rapid gunshots to my left. "Austin!"

A root snags my foot, but I don't go down like some hapless horror movie scream queen. Instead, I leap over a bush and land next to my brother. He's on his ass, panting, holding the gun in both hands. Henrik has taken his shirt off and is wrapping it around Austin's calf.

"I know I got it," Austin says. I flash the beam on his face. He's pale as milk, his eyes beginning to glaze.

"What happened?" I ask Henrik.

"It lashed out with its tail. Swept him off his feet, but he never stopped firing. He's right, he did get it." He cinches the shirt on the wound. There's so much rain, it's hard to gauge how much blood Austin's lost.

"I know I did. I didn't miss."

"Let me check." I walk toward the water. The slip is only a twenty or so yards away.

"Don't go alone," Henrik says.

It's too late for that. I'm scared witless, but I can't stop my legs from going deeper into the dark, right where those things were headed. Maybe I am the dumb blonde scream queen after all.

I sweep the light back and forth, eyes on the ground because I'm pretty damn sure they won't be hiding in the trees. I hold the gun in my other hand, worrying that if I have to shoot, will it have a kick that'll knock me on my ass?

There are fading ripples in the water, a rapidly fading marker pointing to their escape.

Then I see it, wet and bloody and reeking like a month old fish fry.

Henrik and Austin catch up to me.

I keep the flashlight on the bizarre parting gift. "You got it all right."

CHAPTER EIGHTEEN

We carry what one of the Loch Ness Monsters left behind in a tarp. Rainwater rapidly fills the little bowl, sloshing over the sides. Some of it gets on my shoes. I'm going to have to throw those sneakers out. No way that funk is ever coming out of them.

"Let's get it inside so we can have a better look," Austin says. He's limping, but it's not slowing him down. He's way too jazzed to even feel the pain.

"No way, Jose. Not in my house."

Henrik starts to unwind the awning outside. "It is a bit...repugnant, Austin. I have a lantern in my van."

He dips inside to get his keys. I grab a folding chair for Austin to sit down.

"Here, pop a squat. Take some pressure off your leg."

"Nah, I'm good. It was just a scratch."

Henrik's T-shirt is dyed crimson. Blood is leaking in little rivers down his leg.

"Yeah, a scratch from a twenty-foot monster. Sit."

Henrik arrives with a battery-powered lantern that could light up a gymnasium. I have to shield my eyes for a moment. When I open them, Austin is still standing. Do big brothers ever listen to their little sisters?

We stare at the dismembered flipper for what seems like hours in stunned silence. I can't take my eyes off it. Those sharp finger thingies make me want to hurl.

Austin pokes at it with the tip of his sneaker. "The big question is, is it technically surf, or turf?"

Henrik squats close to it, pulls a pen from his pocket, and prods the gray, splotchy flesh.

"If it were a steak on the grill, I'd call it well done. The musculature here is incredible." He offers the pen to me. I hold back my gorge and give it a try. Even through the pen, it feels as if the flipper is made of Kevlar.

Although the series of bullets that tore it free from its body say otherwise.

"How in the hell did you manage to do this?"

Austin shakes his head. "Lucky shots. I was just shooting as fast as I could before they got away."

"Annie Oakley should have been so lucky."

Henrik takes the lantern and walks away from the flipper, lighting up the ground filled with cow bodies. "I wonder if they'll come back for it."

"Even dumb animals are smart enough not to return to the place they got fragged," Austin says. He finally takes a seat, his eyes glued to his prize.

Something that's been bothering me since they showed up at my doorstep needs to be said. "I wonder if they found this place because of all the fresh, odiferous meat we have lying around, or if they tracked my boat. Because if they can track my boat, they're going to know when we're coming."

I can tell it hits it a nerve with my brother and Henrik. The three of us stand in the rain, oblivious to the fact that we're getting soaked, that Austin needs medical attention, that we're surrounded by rotting meat and are now in the possession of a Loch Ness Monster flipper.

Henrik tilts the tarp so the rancid water runs into the dirt, making sure not to get any on us. He wraps the flipper like a tidy Christmas present and secures it to the rack on the roof of his van with some rope. He then moves the van so it's downwind of us.

Again. Boy Scout. Many badges.

"Help me get Mr. Atlas inside."

"I told you, I'm fine."

Austin steps into the RV leaving a little trail of blood droplets.

"Go straight to the bathroom, please. And try not to ruin my carpet."

He sits on the toilet while I take the T-shirt off his leg. The meaty furrow in his calf looks like the San Andrea fault line. He tries to push the edges closed, which only make more blood seep out.

I have to back out of the bathroom. I just saw the raw chop-meat of his leg. I swear everything tonight is conspiring to get me to lose my dinner.

Henrik takes a quick look and says he has to go back out to the van. He comes back with a professional grade first-aid kit in a black plastic case. He starts threading a curved needle.

"Natalie, can you pour the disinfectant on his leg, please?"

I unscrew the cap and look my brother in the eye. "You're not going to cry like a little girl are you?"

"Just do it and see for yourself."

There is a sharp intake of breath and his body goes rigid for a few seconds, but he doesn't cry. The disinfectant bubbles the moment it hits the gaping wound.

"I don't have anything to numb you," Henrik says, looking like a tailor about to mend a suit.

"You have everything but that? I can't catch a break."

Henrik squeezes the bottom end of the ragged slash and Austin's eye bug out of his skull. I can hear his skin pop when the needle goes in. I cover my mouth with my hand.

"I think you caught a break when it didn't hit any major arteries. Please don't move. It'll only make this take longer and make the scar worse."

Crushing a roll of toilet paper, Austin's already pasty complexion goes a whiter shade of pale. "It's not the scar I'm concerned about."

I remember I have a bottle of whiskey in the cabinet. I give the whole thing to Austin. He takes a deep chug.

Henrik pauses his mending to take the bottle out of his hands. "Alcohol will only thin his blood and make clotting even more difficult. When I'm done, he can have some Ibuprofen."

"Ibuprofen? You out of children's chewable aspirin?"

Henrik hands me the bottle. Austin gives me the puppy dog eyes, made even more pathetic by the pain swimming in them.

Without looking up from his work, Henrik says, "Don't you dare."

I don't dare.

I somehow think the stitches would have been easier if Austin hadn't gone all muscle bound. Henrik is sewing up the outer layers of his skin, not his muscle, though I'll never get the image of said exposed muscle out of my head. When it's over, Austin's lays his head back and smiles.

"That was fun."

Henrik tidies up his first-aid kit. "I believe I'll take this on the boat with us tomorrow."

"You mean today," I remind him, pointing at the lightening skies outside my cracked window.

"That damn thing's tail was like a whip," Austin says, hobbling to his makeshift bed. "I just hope it wasn't radioactive or laced with some kind of toxic waste. I could be changing into a monster as we speak, or melting from the inside out."

"If you start to melt, do me a kindness and take it outside. I have plans to sell this RV when we're done, and I've already lost resale value from the pounding it took."

Henrik runs his fingertips along the network of fine cracks in the window. "I wonder why they didn't just take the food and run. It's as if they wanted us to know they were here."

"Or even worse," I say, "they smelled a live after-dinner snack and wanted in."

CHAPTER NINETEEN

I find what is surely an expired Xanax and give it to Austin so he can catch a few more Zs. We need him to be strong later. Whatever downtime he can get to recover is vitally necessary.

There's been a pause in the rain, but the weather forecast calls for a rapid return of the great and welcome deluge by late morning. Henrik is outside, studying the flipper. It looks and smells like it's already rotting. The color is leaching from the flesh, crinkling like old, wet paper.

"It's as big as my torso," he says.

"It would have to be to propel that body. Any chance you can count rings to determine how old it is?"

"No, but I can count my blessings that we're all still here. I don't like surprises."

Leaning back against the RV, I drink from a mug of tepid coffee. "I should have taken what Rob told us and used my head. If the food supply is getting low, which by all indications it's pretty bad right now, they're going to go wherever they have to go to feed. Since we know they can live on land, at least for a short period of time, I should have had the foresight to at least have us take watches, knowing we have a damn seven-course meal sitting outside."

I can't help feeling like an idiot. I'd spent all these years dreaming and preparing for a confrontation with the monsters that took our parents from us. But those dreams and plans always included being on the water.

"The beasts of man's nightmares have no care for his aspirations or expectations." He folds up Austin's booty, agitating a swarm of flies.

"That's actually very nice. Where's it from?"

He doesn't put the flipper back on his van. Instead, he sets the tarp next to one of the carcasses. "*The Collected Improvisational Works of Henrik Kooper*. The latest edition just came out ten seconds ago. Critics are raving."

Henrik always seems so in control, so calm, so…Zen. I hope that veneer doesn't crack later on. I think we're going to need his steady head as much as his cache of what Austin calls *weapons of monster destruction.*

"Tell me, if you weren't hunting Loch Ness Monsters or Orang Pendeks, what would you be doing?" I toss the dregs of the coffee on the ground and check my watch. It's just about time for me to get one last and one new task completed.

"Back home, I do photography. Art house stuff, not family portraits in a mall. I have a couple of works at small galleries. I'll show you someday."

"I'd like that."

I'm still astounded by how quickly I've come to trust this man. It goes beyond the bond shared by two people who lost someone they loved to a monster. Or does it? Maybe whatever forces thrust us into the impossible are also at work bringing us together.

'Well, me and Eileen have to bop into town for a few. You should try to get as much rest as you can, too."

He gives me a slight bow with a flourish of his hands. "Is there anything I can do to help?"

"You'll have plenty to do…later."

I hop into my VW Bug and roll down the windows to take advantage of the fresh, dry air while it lasts. As I pull away, I hear Henrik call after me, "Who is Eileen?"

I'd explain that Eileen is Shania Twain's real name, but I doubt that will even make things any clearer. I head up the dirt road blasting a little *Whose Bed Have Your Boots Been Under,* wishing Austin was in the passenger seat so I could torture him on the drive to town.

I throw Mrs. Carr off her game when I walk into her shop and immediately ask, "How can I get in touch with Billy Firth?"

She looks as if I just asked if I can give her an apple cider enema.

"Oh, dear, the weather is dreadful. Not a good day to rent Billy's boat."

I'm worried that maybe there never was a Billy Firth, or if there was, he's been dead for several decades, a ghost from Mrs. Carr's past that refuses to fade away.

"It's not raining now. I figured I'd see if he's willing to part with his boat for a little while."

She motions for me to come closer and takes my hands in her own. They feel so fragile and soft as suede. "Only if you promise me you'll head right back the moment the weather gets unsettled. I don't want to carry the burden of guilt should something happen to you."

I instantly regret coming here. The odds are pretty high that something untoward will happen to me, with or without Billy Firth's boat. Knowing she'll feel guilty no matter what makes me feel like a world class ass for opening my big mouth.

Choking on my lie, I reply, "I promise. I'm no big time lake explorer. I just want to take advantage of things on a day when I'll have it mostly to myself."

The old lady grins, patting my hand. "That's a good girl. And when you come back, I received a new box of paperbacks yesterday. I've set it aside so you can go through it first and see what catches your fancy."

She gives me directions to Billy Firth's place and I thank her profusely, telling her I can't wait to rummage through the books.

And now a conundrum. If my plan gets out of hand and we have to light out of the Highlands in a hurry, do I still stop to look at the books and say goodbye to the sweetest woman I've ever known at the risk of being caught?

I look back and she's waving from the register, even though I know for sure she can't see me.

Henrik and Austin may just have to go on an Orang Pendek hunt by themselves.

To my surprise, Billy Firth is alive and well.

Okay, alive.

He's not much older than me, but in sorry shape. He answers the door wearing an oxygen mask. He's a husky guy, if you define husky as someone weighing close to three bills. I explain that Mrs. Carr said he might have a boat to rent.

Riding a red scooter, he leads me to the dock behind his house.

"I don't have much call for using it myself," he says, coughing into the plastic mask, fogging it up. "Once my back went, the rest followed. I have a lad who stops by every week to make sure she's kept clean and running. Not many potential renters coming my way, but I want her ready for when I get out of this scooter. Only a little left to lose before I qualify for the bypass surgery."

As the folks over here would say, I'm gobsmacked to see a thirty-foot cigarette boat in pristine condition. It's yellow as the sun, that orb I haven't seen in a while, and looks like a water rocket, which it is. Cigarette boats are built for speed.

Billy says, "She has a fiberglass hull and twin outboard engines that make you feel as if you're flying over the loch rather than riding on it. You ever driven one before?"

Since the lies are coming so easily, I say, "Yeah, quite a few times."

He pulls the mask away from his face. "You're from America, aren't you?"

"Born and bred. Spent a lot of time in Florida. Cigarette boats were all the rage when I was growing up."

Now, I've been to Florida once, when my aunt took Austin and me to Disney World. The closest we came to riding in a boat was on the log flume ride.

"How much for the day if bring it back tomorrow morning?"

If there is a tomorrow morning. And a boat to bring back.

He gives me a price that is this side of gouging. It doesn't take a genius to see he needs the money. Even his scooter looks like it needs a scooter. I almost give him heart failure to add to his woes by telling him I'll pay double.

"I don't understand."

"I'll need someone to bring it to me this morning. I don't want to leave my car here. Do you think the lad who keeps her shipshape could do it?" I hand him a considerable wad of cash. He holds it in his hand and stares at it.

"That little bit of service hardly seems worth what you're paying."

I place my hand on his shoulder. It's doughy and sweaty. "That surgery is expensive. You do what you have to do and get back on your feet."

Does one good deed counteract two bald lies?

I doubt it, but it'll have to do for now.

CHAPTER TWENTY

Austin and Henrik have a breakfast made for Midwestern mommas at a free Vegas buffet waiting for me when I return. Basically, they've cooked up everything in the RV. There's bacon and toast, chicken curry and white rice, a bowl of steaming tomato soup, scrambled eggs, sausage, a wedge salad, rolls, and mushy peas. The whole last meal comparison isn't lost on me.

"I thought that pill would knock you out for longer."

Austin escorts me to my seat. He's walking better than before.

"Nothing can put me down. Henrik is the one who started frying everything up. It was impossible to sleep through the smell of bacon."

Henrik waves a spatula. "My apologies, Natalie."

"None needed. I didn't realize how hungry I am until I walked in here." Despite my brain telling me it's breakfast and I'm supposed to eat breakfast things, I pile the chicken curry on my plate.

There's a knock at the door and Austin answers. Fidgety Rob Rayman is right on time.

"Smells delicious."

"Grab a plate and sit down." I motion for him to take one of the comfy front seats. He can balance the plate on the center console.

We tear into the food like starved jackals. We grunt, we *mmmm* and *ahhh*, but that's the full extent of our verbal powers.

Austin eats so many eggs, I know I don't want to be downwind of him later. "What's with all the eggs?"

"Protein. It's all about protein."

It must be at that, because his plate is all meat and eggs.

Rob, I notice, is all about the carbs. I knew I liked him for a reason.

Once we finish our gluttony, my stomach so full and tight it's hard to breathe, I ask Rob, "You have all your stuff?"

"Every last recording device. And that's a lot." He keeps dabbing at his forehead with his napkin, blotting out a spot only he can see.

"Good. You'll need all of it. You're going to be our eyes on the land, but we're going to have to make sure you're protected."

"Protected?" Some crumbs fall from the corners of his mouth onto his lap.

I explain what happened last night. He keeps licking his lips. I can't tell if he's excited, nervous or if it simply means nothing.

To ease any fears, I add, "Look, I'm sure you'll be fine. They came here because they wanted what's outside. It'll all be in the water later, so they'll have no need to head for dry land."

I leave out my theory that they may have been there to hurt or eat us rather than stealing a cowhide or two. A lie of omission. I'm on a roll today.

Henrik hands Rob what looks an awful lot like an Uzi. I've seen enough Rambo and Bruce Willis movies to know.

Rob visibly recoils. "I'm a pacifist."

Henrik puts the Uzi in his lap. "If one of those creatures approaches you, I guarantee you'll change your moral stance."

"But I've never even held a gun before. It's really heavy."

"The good news for you is this is not a gun. All you need to do is pull the trigger and hold it down. The bullets will handle the rest. The creatures are too big to miss."

Austin clasps his hands behind his head, leaning back in his chair. "Even if you're firing practically blind in the dark. Once you've digested a little bit, I'll show you."

Rob looks understandably confused.

"I...I thought I'm just here to take pictures. I already have reservations about your intentions. I didn't plan on being part of a small army."

It looks like every nerve in his body is crawling to make a break. Poor guy. Maybe I shouldn't have let him in on everything. But it's too late now. I take the seat next to him and rest a hand on his lap. I can feel his muscles twitching.

"We just want you to be safe. Those things are wild animals. It's impossible to get inside their heads and know what they're going to do, how they'll react. So we just have to prepare for the worst. My parents had a bomb shelter under our house growing up. It was fully stocked with enough food and water, board games, and medical supplies to last several months. It scared me as a kid, because a bomb shelter meant there was the possibility of bombs dropping from the sky. But they never did, and eventually, the food went bad and the water evaporated."

Henrik scowls. "You should always rotate supplies and buy new when necessary."

I can't help shaking my head at him. "Anyway, the point is, a little prep work never hurt anyone. And ninety-nine percent of the time, you'll never even use the stuff."

Rob looks down at the Uzi like it's a hungry honey badger. "How can I operate my cameras and carry this thing around at the same time?"

Henrik produces a leather strap from his pocket. "With this."

The rain has returned, plinking on the RVs hull. I can also hear the hum of what can only be my special delivery. "I'll be right back."

I change into the waterproof jogging suit. When Henrik sees me, his face lights up with approval. "Don't say a word," I warn him, exiting the RV.

Billy's helper is wearing a dirty yellow slicker. A friend followed him over in a small Sunray. The kid barely speaks, just asks, "You know what you're doing?"

I lie yet again. "Of course. Thanks for the door to door service." I slip him a very nice tip. He doesn't even look at it. Just shoves it in his pocket and jumps into the Sunray.

"What have we got here?" Austin startles me. He's also in his waterproof suit.

"An escape pod if we need it."

Henrik comes up on the other side of me. In his black suit, we look like the Blue Man Group before makeup. "You're going to tow that?"

I hand him the keys. "You're going to drive it."

"But I don't know how to drive a boat."

I pat his arm as I walk past him, back to the RV where Rob is waiting just inside the open door. "You will after today."

CHAPTER TWENTY-ONE

We spend a quarter of an hour going over a map of Loch Ness.
I explain to Rob where we plan to set our trap and point out the
best and safest spots to position his equipment. He keeps giving
the Uzi furtive glances, as if he's waiting for it to come alive and
demand he lay waste to something…anything.

The storm's intensity rises, which is perfect. The worst is
predicted to settle over the loch in the late afternoon. The worse
the weather gets, the less innocent bystanders that will be out and
about. I have a sneaking suspicion this is going to get very, very
ugly. The only person I want chronicling it is Rob. At least with
him, we'll have some control over the content that's released. The
last thing I want are our faces on the most wanted list. I'm sure
there's some law on the books about killing an unknown beloved
species, no matter how deadly they are.

Unless we discover later that the essential oil of a Loch Ness
Monster cures baldness or improves erections. Then it's open
season on Nessie.

Rob asks if he can have the map, reluctantly picks up the Uzi,
and heads to his car.

Austin and Henrik look tired, but ready to roll.

"Let's prep the bait and get them loaded on Vindicta."

Another good thing about the rain – it's keeping the flies off
the cows. There are too many for me to come up with amusing
names. Bait will do just fine today.

In the long storage area at the back of the RV, I have yards of
chains and orange buoys. We haul it all out, some of the chains

tangling together even though I did everything I could when I put them there to make sure that didn't happen. It's like Christmas lights, or as they say on this side of the Atlantic, fairy lights.

"That is going to make a lot of floaters," Austin says. He's trying hard to mask his limp, but I can tell he's still in pain. I'm tempted to tell him to stay ashore and watch Rob's back. But I know there's nothing I can do keep him off the loch. He's waited just as long as I have for this. Only difference is, he decided to have a life during the wait. Although I can't complain about the life of leisure I've led. Aside from obsessing over the monsters and waking up with night terrors every night, I did read a lot and watched a ton of movies. I'm pretty caught up on the classics and oldies.

"All the better to bring them to the surface, my pretty." I can get the meat ready, but I can't carry it to Vindicta. That's all Austin and Henrik.

"I hope I don't hit into your boat," Henrik says. Vindicta is sitting so low in the water from the extra weight of the weapons and now cow corpses, I can barely see the pontoons.

"You and me both."

I tell them they have to load a few of the cows onto the cigarette boat to lighten the load. My little impromptu addition to the plan is already paying dividends.

The rain is pissing in a non-stop stream, the boats are loaded, and it's finally time. Now that it's here, I go numb for a moment. I know Austin is saying something to me, but I can't make out a word. It feels like I'm having an out of body experience, though I'm not floating somewhere looking at us from above. Every limb is dead weight, my brain unable to formulate the commands to get them to move.

I am looking at the water, waves lapping into a froth at the shore, the rain poking thousands of little holes into the surface.

For a moment, I see my parents, the coiled body of the monster constricting their helpless bodies. They're calling out for me. The look of terror on their faces stops my heart.

"Don't let it take us!" my mother pleads.

I can't move. I can't speak. Not even enough to tell them I love them one final time.

The creature gives one last squeeze and everything that's supposed to be inside a person comes rocketing out of every orifice. It pulls them down into the murk, a crimson oil slick the only thing left in the wake of the attack.

And just like that, it ends. I can feel the rain splashing my face, the lubricated sheen of cow fat on my hands.

"…you want, I can drive the cigarette boat. I've been behind the wheel of a few speedboats when I was down in Mexico."

Austin must sense my temporary slip from reality because he grabs onto my shoulders.

"You all right? You look like you were about to pass out there."

I shake it off. The nightmare, the memory, must know it's coming to an end. It's invaded my waking life, taking one more crack at my sanity.

I feel the heat of my tears spring like a tapped well. I'm hoping Austin can't see them through the steady stream of rain cascading down my face.

"Yeah, yeah, I'm fine. Just got a little light headed for a sec. Must be the methane from the cows."

Austin scratches his head. "I'm pretty sure they need to be alive and flatulating up a storm for that to happen."

I look up at his face, this twin brother who has come back a different man on the outside, but is still the lovable lunkhead on the inside, and I ask him to hug me. He sweeps me off my feet in a bear hug to end all bear hugs.

"I know," he whispers in my ear. "I know."

When he puts me down, I'm more in control of myself. Sometimes you just need a good, quick cry and a hug. Especially when you're moments away from exacting the revenge that has been eating you alive for twenty years.

"Do I get a hug?" Henrik asks Austin.

"No, but how about a hearty pat on the back?"

I get aboard Vindicta. My poor baby. She's already taken a beating. I'm not sure she's going to make it back this time. I vow that when we're done here, and after we help Henrik, I'm going to find a nice lake house in New England, buy another pontoon boat, and call it Vindicta 2.

I'll have to do my research first, make sure there are no stories of lake monsters wherever I decide to settle.

Henrik starts up the cigarette boat with a loud roar. He jumps about two feet off the deck.

"It sounds very powerful," he shouts over to us.

"That's because it is. Just take it slow. It'll ride rougher that way, but I don't want you taking off and crashing. Remember, you're in charge of our escape pod."

An escape pod that's also loaded with weapons. He has no plans on being a casual observer.

"Just follow me, to my starboard. Don't creep up behind me. If you juice it too much, you'll ride over Vindicta like it's a ramp and you're a German Fonzie."

He gives me a shaky thumbs-up. I'll bet he has no clue who Fonzie is.

Maybe I should have had Austin take the cigarette boat, but he's my brother – my twin brother.

We have to do this together.

I pull away from the slip for what I hope is the last time. Austin has a meaty hand on my head as if he's palming a basketball. It used to irritate the crap out of me when we were kids.

My, how things have changed.

The spot I've determined we'll release the bait is eight miles up the loch. I'm anxious as all get out to get there.

Until I hear the screams.

CHAPTER TWENTY-TWO

I turn Vindicta around a spit of land dotted with dead trees and scrub grass. It's a seldom-used fishing spot in the summer because there's no way to get out from under the sun's punishing glare. The Scots are not sun worshippers. At least not the ones I've met. Worse still, the midges swarm it when it's hot out, making it highly uncomfortable. Nothing is more irritating that being covered in those damn midges. One minute is enough to make a person go mad.

There's a rowboat tied to a tree stump, the loch's turgid waters making it dance as if it were in a mosh pit.

The screaming is coming from an older man in hip waders. He's out of the boat, on his ass, scrabbling backwards.

One of the creatures is half-in, half-out of the water, inching toward him.

Inching isn't quite right. It's coming for him at a pretty good clip. As its body clears the water, I see it's one of the creatures from last night's attack on my RV. The man isn't Nessie chow already only because it's having a rough time navigating dry land on just the one flipper.

"There's your buddy."

Austin reaches under the bench and grabs an AR-15. "I guess he was too wounded to get very far."

"Or waiting for us and this poor schmuck just happened to be in the wrong place as the wrong time."

I keep ascribing a cold intelligence to these creatures. For some reason, it's hard for me to think of them as unintelligent animals. To survive this long in relative secrecy requires either an incredible amount of dumb luck or some kind of ability to learn and plan and coordinate.

Austin hops over the side of Vindicta. The water is up to his chest. He holds the assault rifle over his head, careful not to get it wet. We have other weapons onboard specifically designed to work underwater, but the AR-15 isn't one of them.

"Sir, I need you to get out of the way!" Austin barks, fighting through the water.

The creature snaps its jaws at the old man, and instead of moving faster, he freezes.

I can't help but shout, "Get the hell up and run!"

Henrik pulls the cigarette boat alongside me. He has a rifle in his hands, looking down the sight. He takes a shot. There's a sharp crack, and I see a hole bore into the monster's rear end.

It may not be a killing blow, but it gets its attention.

I scream at the man again, "Now! Go! Go! Go!"

Austin is on the bank now, water sluicing off his suit. The monster lashes its tail at him, but he dodges to his left. "Fool me once, bitch."

The old man, counter to anything a rational person would do, heads *toward* the monster in a blind panic.

Henrik puts his rifle down. "What the hell is he doing?"

"I don't know."

I figure his close encounter has literally shattered his brain. Any ability to think clearly is now encased in a fog of numb stupidity.

Then I see exactly what he's doing, and it still doesn't make much sense. "He's going for his boat."

Austin is so fixated by the monster that he doesn't notice the scared witless man dashing alongside its long, sinuous body. He opens up with the AR-15, starting from the head and working his way down with a continuous barrage of armor-piercing bullets.

The Loch Ness Monster bleats like a wounded goat...or more like a hundred wounded goats. Its cries echo over the loch.

Foul flesh and gouts of blood erupt in a meandering line down to its tail. It's like watching little connect the dots magically appear. The creature flips sideways. When it's down but still gyrating, Austin rushes to its head. He steps on its neck and with a roar of his own, he empties the gun into its vile face, reducing it to an oozing mush.

Even without a head, the body still twitches and writes, just like an eel. But despite all of the recent theories that the beast has been some sort of giant eel all along, I can plainly see that's just not true.

I let out a hearty whoop, raising my fist in the air. We've been on the water for less than five minutes and we've already bagged one. Austin looks back at me with an impish grin. He's covered from head to toe in Nessie blood.

Then Henrik says, "Where did that man go?"

The rowboat is still there – empty.

"Austin, the guy, where is he?"

My brother looks confused. He was so busy trying to stay alive himself and kill the beast, he probably didn't notice him at all.

I can hear Henrik groan over the idling of both boats. "I think I see him. Or at least his arm."

I follow where he's pointing and see it, too.

There's just an arm, the fingers locked into a claw.

The rest of him is under the creature. I tell Austin where he is and he hops over the body, sliding down its torso. He crouches down and is out of sight for a few seconds. When he pops up, his body language has completely changed.

"He's gone, Nat. It squashed him flat."

Well, fuck!

CHAPTER TWENTY-THREE

That takes the wind out of our sails.

Austin and I don't speak when he gets back on board. Henrik asks if we should call an ambulance, anonymously, of course. He informs me that he has several burner phones. I tell him it can wait. There's nothing they can do for him now, anyway. We'll call when we're done.

"I killed him."

My brother is sitting on one of the lounge benches, the rifle between his legs, his head hanging low. I can't have him falling apart.

"You didn't. That *thing* killed him."

"I was reckless. I should have been paying attention. I thought saving him was the reason I jumped out of the boat, but now I'm not so sure."

The rain is pelting the awning over us so hard, it sounds like a continuous rumble of thunder.

"You did what you had to do. If he hadn't gone in the wrong direction, he'd be running home right now. You couldn't know he'd do that."

Austin's eyes are red. "But I could have watched out for the guy! Jesus, we didn't come here to get innocent people killed. What would Mom and Dad say?"

The truth is, they've been gone so long, I can barely remember their voices, much less take a stab at their thoughts. I still love them dearly and miss them with every fiber of my being, but aside from the nightmare, my tether to them fades each year like a photograph left out in the sun.

Henrik is doing a good enough job with the cigarette boat. He's not getting so close that I worry about any collisions, but I can clearly see him through the curtain of rain glancing over at us, at Austin specifically. He's as worried as I am. If what just happened causes Austin to hesitate later, it could cost him his life. Or all our lives.

I hate the whole tough love concept. Love is unconditional, not cold. But right now, it might be the only chance we've got.

"You're going to have to forget about it."

He glares at me. "What did you say?"

"I need your head in this, Austin. You have the rest of your life to second guess, to punish yourself. And I'll be there to remind you that none of it was your fault. For now, you have to compartmentalize. Lock it in cold storage. Because if you fuck up and get yourself killed, I'll kill you again. *That's* what Mom and Dad would say."

He opens his mouth to speak, then closes it, tightening his grip on the barrel of the rifle. I can see his muscles flexing under his skintight suit. It's like he's waging a silent war within himself.

When he finally speaks, I almost sag against the wheel with relief.

"You're right. I promise, I'll stow that shit away. You won't have to worry about me."

He looks like he's come out of his fugue. Looks can be deceiving, but Austin is a pretty open book to me.

We have about ten more minutes before we get to the bait drop point. I hope Rob is already there...and safe.

"Good, because I have enough on my hands worrying about myself. Now get that big ass rifle out of sight in case someone happens to see us. I don't want to get arrested before the big dance."

Henrik gooses the cigarette boat's twin engines and spurts ahead of me. It's good he's testing it a bit, getting a feel for her. Boats made for speed work the water like a hot knife through clotted cream. When they're going slow, they're like wartime jeeps on a bombed out road.

I see Rob waving to us from the shore. He's surrounded by cameras mounted on tripods. Looks like he has still and video going. I know there are plenty more set up all over the area, including some strapped to trees to get better angles. It's a relief not to see him being hunted down like today's hot plate special.

"Hang on just a sec," I say, bringing the boat to the shore. I jump into the water that goes past my waist. Henrik's suit does the trick, keeping me nice and dry. Carrying a rope, I walk to the rocky bit of land and tie it off on a tree limb.

Rob keeps sucking his lower lip in, then letting it out. He's as nervous as a kid on his first day of kindergarten.

"I thought I heard gunfire," he says.

"Damn. I was hoping it wouldn't carry this far. We ran across one of the creatures back there. It was on land."

Rob's eyes go wide. "Another one on land?"

"Afraid so. It was the same one that attacked my RV. At least I'm pretty sure it was." I look around the little video studio he's set up. "Where's your Uzi?"

He points to a black plastic case. The case has a tripod and video camera sitting on it.

"I really need you to make sure you have it on you. Not buried under equipment."

"Natalie, I just don't think…"

I cut him off by raising my hand, and my voice. "I'm not asking you to think. Just do it. There was a man fishing back there. The creature came out of the water to eat him. I can't do what I have to do if I don't feel you're taking every precaution."

Ron walks over to the case, gently removing the tripod.

"Is the man who was fishing all right?"

I try to hide the inevitable sigh. This time, I'm not going to lie. "No, Rob. He's dead. The thing rolled over on him. But Austin managed to kill it."

He looks like he's going to throw up. I give him time to collect himself. "Look, you can just get your stuff and go back to your camp. Stay safe. I'm not going to force you to do this."

I hope he heeds my advice. I'm now very concerned for the little, nervous man.

Instead, he stands a little straighter, tapping the side of the Uzi.

"I think I'll stay. You let me in on something bigger than both of us. If I walked away now, I'd be throwing away all the years I spent waiting for a moment like this. Look, I know you're worried, but I'll take care of myself. I really appreciate this. I won't let you guys down."

I bring Rob in for a hug.

"You better take care of yourself," I say.

I wade back in the water and Austin pulled me onto the boat.

"Everything all right?"

I look back at Rob, who's back checking all of his equipment, the deadly gun bouncing off his hip.

"Jesus, I hope so."

Turning Vindicta to the middle of the loch, we stop a few hundred yards from shore.

"We're here. Your big boy muscles up to unloading all this Grade D beef?"

I try to help Austin, but he doesn't let me. It would be easiest to just push them over the side of the boat, but he elects for a clean and jerk, followed by a cow toss. They hit the water with a tremendous splash, the bodies and the buoys going completely under for a moment. I worry that we didn't chain them up tight enough and the carcasses are slipping free, sinking to the bottom where they'll do us no good.

I breathe again when the buoys bob to the surface.

"You okay over there, Henrik?"

The cigarette boat isn't designed so he can easily push or flip the bait over the side. He's struggling to get the first one up and over. When it does slip out of his hands, diving into the dingy loch, his black suit is smeared with cow goo. He looks down in disgust.

I tell him, "The rain will take care of that."

"Yeah, just don't go for a quick dip," Austin adds, manhandling the fourth hunk of bait over Vindicta.

Grunt. Splash. Grunt. Splash. The sounds are repeated over and over until everything's in the pool. Vindicta feels infinitely lighter, which is very good, because it's not a stretch to think she'll be motoring her ass off at some point today.

I call Rob on my cell phone.

"You all set?"

I picture him shaking his head rapidly, like a prairie dog with a case of the yips. "Anything that happens out there will be captured six ways to Sunday."

I'm tempted to ask if it matters that it's Wednesday, but he doesn't seem like he'd get the joke. Levity is in short supply about now. His voice is tight and I know his nerves are on a razor's edge.

I'm sure the windfall that will come his way later will more than pay for any therapy he needs to get right with the world again. Maybe we can get a two-for-one deal with a shrink.

The orange buoys bob violently on the loch. The wind's picked up. The water is nothing but whitecaps.

"We should load up," Austin says, lifting the lounge cushion. So many shiny weapons. At least we know they work. We also position the depth charges around Vindicta so it will be easy to deploy them when the time comes.

Henrik says, "The water is so choppy, they're going to have to breach the surface for us to know they're going for the bait."

He's right. Every buoy has the appearance of being tugged on from beneath. For all we know, there could be a Loch Ness Monster feast going on below our feet. I'm betting those big boys and girls are going to churn things up considerably when they get to feeding. We'll know when they're here, all right.

All three of us have strapped Bullpup rifles across our chests. They're made for amphibious shooting. I insisted we do it just in case things get rocky and someone goes overboard. Or if Austin decides to play Tarzan again. We can't be in the drink with no way to defend ourselves.

The strap is cutting my cleavage something fierce, but I have to suck it up. Not having it is not an option.

As far as I can see, there isn't another boat on the loch or person by the shores, other than Rob. I'm sure there might be another fisherman or two about, but the Loch is huge and I just pray they're nowhere near here.

"Come on, you hungry little butt wipes. The restaurant is all yours."

The buoys are starting to scatter, tossed by the roiling current. I'm worried that they'll spread across an area too wide to control. It's great that we have privacy, but it's coming at the cost of...

"There it goes!" Austin shouts, pointing to our port side. I turn just in time to see one of the buoys slip completely under. We wait a few beats. It doesn't pop back up. "One of them must be munching on it right now."

I hope it's tearing in like Henry VIII on a turkey leg. What those creatures don't know is that we made small cuts throughout all of the carcasses, filling each with what look like tiny jacks, except all of the points are razor sharp. If they somehow chew through the bait without cutting up their mouths, the barbed surprises will surely wreak havoc on their internal systems.

Austin and I have our AR-15s pointed at the spot where the buoy was last seen. Henrik has something much, much bigger in his hands.

"What is that?"

His face breaks out in a wolfish smile. "Just a grenade launcher."

So much for keeping things on the down low, at least at the start.

There's an explosion of water behind us.

We spin around, ready to blast whatever we see straight to hell.

We're not prepared for this particular sight.

CHAPTER TWENTY-FOUR

I'm literally catching rain in my open mouth as I watch the meat missile soar twenty feet in the air. It's headed straight for the scrub-choked shore, and possibly one of Rob's cameras.

I must be right, because I can even hear Rob wailing, "No, no, no, no!"

It crashes through the branches of a tree and lands with a wet thud, out of sight but definitely not out of mind. It also demolishes a video camera and tripod.

Austin fires a few rounds into the water, even though we can't see anything. "I guess that's their way of sending the food back to the chef."

"How the fuck did it do that?"

I never counted on the Nessies rejecting the bait. Ignoring it, maybe. But never this.

"Another one just disappeared," Henrik calmly calls out. We turn around again. One, now two more buoys are dragged under. Austin and I fire away, hoping one of them is close enough to the surface to catch some lead.

We stop when we realize we're just wasting ammo.

"Guess they liked those," I say.

Me and my big mouth.

A carcass flies out from the depths, this time taking a lazy arc to our left and splattering back into the loch. We're so busy watching it, we're not prepared for the next one that clips one of Vindicta's pontoons as it makes its improbable journey to the gray skies. The boast tips backward and we both fall hard.

I'm up on my feet first. "Crap, they're using them as weapons against us."

Austin grabs one of the depth charges and activates it. "We'll see how they like this."

"Austin, no!"

He's too fast and I'm too late. The depth charge hits the water and immediately starts sinking.

All I can think of is, *what if they toss that back, too?*

"I know what you're worrying about and you don't need to."

Twin power at work.

"And why is that?"

The explosion rocks the boat, a great plume of big white bubbles coming up for air.

Austin grins. "Short fuse."

"Get ready," Henrik says.

Waiting for a body to float up feels like forever. It never comes.

And no more buoys are disappearing, either.

"Crap, we scared them off."

Austin waves his rifle back and forth over the water, ready to let fly. "I think it'll take more than that."

Henrik disagrees. "If they use any type of natural sonar for their navigation, the depth charge will have set them off in any direction. They may not even know where they're going, except away from here."

Rob is standing at the shore with his hands cupped around his mouth. I can barely hear him. Why doesn't he just use his cell phone? We're being shocked dumb by these creatures.

Henrik pulls around us to get closer. "It was a depth charge!" he has to shout back at Rob.

I don't need to see his face to know there's a mask of befuddlement. I mean, how many people can get their hands on depth charges?

Taking a quick peek over the side of Vindicta, I see a fresh dent in one of the pontoons, a la the dangerous trajectory of the meat rocket. I'll have to write the manufacturer and thank them for making them so sturdy. I'm sure something like this was never anticipated in their stress tests.

"Well, this sucks. And I know someone had to hear that thing go off." I'm very worried that our mission has ended before it even began. And all Rob has to show for his efforts are flying cows. It could go viral on YouTube, but I'm pretty damn sure that's not what he had in mind when he joined our merry hunting party.

But there is still the dead body atop the fisherman, if one of its brethren hasn't come up and taken it away. At this point, I'll believe just about anything.

"I'm sorry, Nat. I just thought since they were so close, I could take a few of them out with one shot."

I pat Austin's chest. It feels like slapping the side of a building. "Hey, that's why we have them. I was hoping that would work, too. So long as they didn't regurgitate it back at us. That's a partial win."

"Uh, McQueens."

Henrik is staring with wide eyes at the loch.

I'm instantly elated and terrified.

All of the buoys are gone.

The monsters didn't leave.

They were just reloading.

CHAPTER TWENTY-FIVE

I hate it when I'm right.

The remaining bait spew from beneath the loch simultaneously – over half a dozen deadly projectiles shot straight into the air.

And what goes up must come down.

Henrik guns the cigarette boat and is able to tear ass out of the splatter zone in seconds. Austin helplessly watches them rise, crest, and start to fall.

"Get us the hell out of here, Nat!"

I dare to look up. A pontoon boat is not a cigarette boat. What it lacks in speed it makes up for in stability. Stability we don't need so much at the moment. We won't make it out of the radius of falling bait in time. I give it all I've got anyway.

I hear the first one splash into the water to my right.

Don't think about it. Just keep going.

Then Austin says the one thing I did not want to hear.

"Incoming!"

He tackles me from behind, tearing my hands from the wheel, his big body covering me as I'm pinned to the floor.

The bait hits Vindicta so hard and loud, I'm sure she's broken in two. It's like a fat kid who plops onto one end of a seesaw. Austin and I are catapulted off the deck. I flail my legs and arms to no avail. I see my boat below me. It looks like it's speeding in the opposite direction, but it's Austin and me who are moving away.

His weight is lifted off me. I can't see where he is. I can only hope when I hit the water, I don't land on top of him. My Bullpup rifle is at my back. If I crash into him rifle first, it may kill him, or at least knock him our cold, which will then cause him to drown.

Funny, and a bit encouraging, that as my own life is flashing before my eyes, I'm only worried about Austin. That should count for something when I approach that big bouncer in the sky, St. Peter. Right?

My body makes a half turn and all I see is the water rushing up to greet me. I hit it with the mother of all belly flops. The water has the consistency of concrete. I lose my breath, and quite possibly my lungs, as I sink like a stone.

It's so dark under the water I can't see. Or am I dead already? Shouldn't there be a light?

My diaphragm starts hitching and my body is craving to draw a breath.

Now I'm panicking and only thinking about myself.

The pain is so extreme, it would be easy to let it overwhelm me, take me under, so to speak. If I'm lucky, I'll drown in my sleep.

Something nudges my leg.

The water is so cold.

Kick your legs, dummy! Paddle your arms! Got to get some air!

Despite the burning in my entire torso, I fight, my hands cupping the water, pulling myself to where I hope the surface is. I'm so disoriented and it's so incredibly dingy down here, I could be swimming deeper, signing my own death warrant.

My legs thrash about.

What just touched my foot?

Why the hell am I even down here?

Shut up. Need...air!

Something feels heavy at my back. I freak. I know it's holding me back.

Oh God, it hurts. I'm going to inhale. Can't stop my body from doing what comes naturally. I know if I do, I'm as good as dead, but my lungs won't listen to reason.

Kick and paddle. Kick and paddle.

It's too far. I've taken a wrong turn. I'll never make it.

And then it happens. My face breaches the surface the second I can no longer fight my instincts. I gulp the air greedily, each inhalation bringing pleasure with equal measures of pain.

A wave washes over me, filling my mouth with water. I rise again, sputtering, choking.

Fighting the chop, I keep my head above water long enough to regain my wits.

"Give me your hand."

Someone's talking to me but I can't see them. Where's Austin?

"Natalie. Turn around. Natalie!"

I make a quick turn, see Henrik stretched over the bow of the cigarette boat, his hand reaching out for me. I lunge for it and he grabs my wrist hard.

"Now your other hand."

I flail and miss. My arms are so numb. Trying to get them to do my bidding is like herding cats.

"Where's…my brother?"

"Safe on board. Now, try again."

I flop my arm forward and Henrik catches it. He starts to pull and I'm halfway out of the water. Jesus, he's strong for such a skinny guy.

I can see Austin. He's lying on the deck, unconscious.

Please don't let him be dead.

"Almost there."

I want to cry with relief. Each breath is a gift. Henrik will take care of me.

I'm hammered from behind. My spine feels like someone took a baseball bat to it. My body goes slack. I know I'm just dead weight.

"No!" Henrik shouts.

My wet wrists slip free from his iron grip. I fall back into the water. Now I hurt in the front and back.

Those monsters aren't about to let me go. They've got me right where they want me, on their home turf. We've got their number on land, but we're no match for them in the loch. I feel so foolish for thinking I could be their executioner.

The Bullpup rifle!

That's what was at my back before. Fully underwater, I reach for the rifle, slinging it over my shoulder.

I can't see a damn thing. But I can pull a trigger.

One...two...three...four...five shots zip through the water. I hear a low, throaty cry. It reverberates through my battered chest, a pulsing weight on my ears.

I hope it hurts like a mother.

Need air.

I head for the surface. Henrik grabs me by the back of my waterproof suit. The rifle is still under the water. I keep pulling the trigger until I'm up and onto the boat.

Henrik lays me next to Austin, though I can sit up.

"Is he...?"

"He's alive."

He grabs the grenade launcher and lets one fly. The water mushrooms. I can hear one of those things screech.

"Our original estimates may have been a bit conservative," Henrik says, eyes on the water.

"Huh?" Everything is a bit fuzzy at the moment.

"About the number of creatures that could survive here."

I pull myself up. Every cell in my body hurts.

Looking around us, I wish I stayed down.

We were wrong.

Oh, so very wrong.

CHAPTER TWENTY-SIX

The fucking things are everywhere. They're in the water. They're on the shore. One of them is lying on its side by the boat. It looks dead. I pray it's dead.

"We underestimated them," Henrik says, letting another grenade fly toward a hump undulating atop the water about forty yards away. It makes a direct hit, shredding the creature's back like pork at a southern barbecue. Its head rears to the surface, obsidian eyes directing all of its hate and pain at us.

I fire at it with the underwater rifle.

Henrik hands me an assault rifle instead. "You'll need this."

There must be twenty of the monsters. It's hard to tell with them in constant motion. Some are on the bank, gobbling the sides of beef they ejected.

"Where's Rob?"

"I haven't seen him."

I fire at anything that moves, hoping Rob is laying low and doesn't wander across my sights.

So much for stealth. Even over the storm, a deaf person could hear the racket we're making.

Henrik says, "I'd kill for a depth charge right about now."

I scan the water for Vindicta. She's floated away from the fray. At least she's still on this side of the water.

All of the depth charges are on Vindicta.

I say, "The genie wants to know if you have another wish."

A hand on my shoulder startles me and my shot goes wild.

"I take a little nap and this is what happens?"

I'm beyond relieved to see Austin awake and on his feet, but I wonder how long it will be before those things overturn the cigarette boat and finish us off like circus peanuts.

"Grab a gun, muscle man."

Henrik covers our back while Austin and I do what we can. The water is rippled with mini explosions. It's hard to tell if we hit them or not. The one Henrik nailed with the grenade floats to the top, a spreading pool of blood coloring the loch.

"Is Rob okay?" Austin asks between shots.

"I don't know. You take the water, I'll concentrate on the shore."

I find a smaller one munching on the bait. I pull the trigger. The shot goes wide, shattering the trunk of a tree. It stops, head turning right to me.

It starts to slink into the water, mouth open wide, emitting a sound that's a cross between a sea lion and a tiger. Must be its war cry.

Taking a deep breath, I let it out and squeeze the trigger again. In the AR-15's sights, I see the bullet carve right into its throat. Its long neck flops back violently. The body is still moving, but now the head is hanging at an unsightly angle, bobbing against its mottled neck.

Dead but forgot to fall.

It slides easily into the water and disappears. I can only hope the wound is fatal.

"Nice shooting."

The water quakes as Henrik sets another grenade loose.

I hear the pop, pop, pop of another gun.

Austin points to the shore. "Look!"

Rob is alive.

But he's not well. He's bleeding from his head. He's covered in so much sanguine gore, he looks like the devil himself.

Rob approaches a feeding creature with unsteady steps, the stumbling gait of a sleepwalker. He doesn't see the one creeping up behind him. Before we can shout a warning, it flicks its tail and sweeps him off his feet. When he hits the ground, the gun goes off, firing impotently into the gray sky.

Henrik takes the rifle from my hands, lifts it to his shoulders, and fires. The creature bellows, twitching away from Rob.

Now the one Rob was intending to shoot sees a fresh meal, not day-old beef. My friend and Nessie hunter is barely moving. He's either out or too dazed to know he's about to die.

Henrik is a good shot, but even he must know it's too risky to take. The creature lowers its head and sniffs at Rob.

"Get us to Vindicta," Henrik says.

I stumble to take control of the cigarette boat, my eyes unable to leave poor Rob.

"Do something."

I realize that even if he accidentally shoots Rob, it would be a mercy. Better that than being eaten alive. I know. I've seen and heard it. It'll probably be the last thing I remember right before I die.

Which could be any minute now.

CHAPTER TWENTY-SEVEN

As I swing the cigarette boat around, I see something that even on a day like today shocks me.

Rob must have been playing dead…or dazed. The moment the creature straddles him, opening its mouth to take a chunk of the Loch Ness Monster hunter, Rob shoves a tripod down its gaping maw, rising up and driving it as deep as possible.

The beast flies backward, flailing about, unable to dislodge the tripod. We can hear it's choking gasps.

Now free, Rob turns to us, gives us a sharp salute, and runs into the deep foliage and out of sight.

Austin whistles in admiration. "Didn't see that coming. Rob Rayman, monster slayer."

Able to breathe again, I hurry to my beloved and embattled pontoon boat. "So much for being a pacifist."

It seems that both man and beast had taken a pause to watch what would happen on the shore. Now that the monster is in its death throes and the puny human beat feet, the Loch Ness Monstrosities, as I now think of them, return their attentions to us. A massive tail breaches the water, swinging for our heads.

"Duck!" I shout.

We all do, which is why we still have something big and round at the end of our necks.

"It didn't do that by accident," Henrik says. "It has to have the power of forethought and planning for a maneuver like that."

The boat bumps the hull of Vindicta. "Yeah, yeah, these things are smarter than the average bear. Let's see if they can figure out how to disarm the depth charges."

I'm contemplating the apparent danger of hopping from one boat to the next, seeing the swells of creatures headed our way, when Austin leaps before he looks. Luckily, he lands on his feet, but the deck is slick with rainwater and he ends up sliding. He has to grab hold of a rail to stop from slipping overboard.

"Asshole." All those muscles must be taking vital blood away from his brain.

"I'm fine," he says, crawling on his hands and knees to one of the depth charges. "Tell me when they're close."

Henrik has an assault rifle now and is unloading it on the approaching monstrosities. I see more lifeless bodies in the water, but we have a long way to go.

I shout back, "Drop it now!"

Austin kicks the depth charge overboard. The humps that have been making headway toward us suddenly stop and change direction. I can feel and hear the explosive detonate. It's followed by a mushroom of water.

Henrik's rifle stops barking and falls to his side. "They knew what was coming."

We watch them gathering fifty yards from us. The ones on land have slithered back into the loch. I'm too afraid to count how many are left. Whatever the number is, it's too damn many.

"We're fucked."

Henrik leaps onto Vindicta. "Not yet. Austin, help me. Natalie, stay on the boat."

He flips open every compartment on my pontoon boat, exposing the cache of weapons we stowed onboard. Some he hands to Austin, who grabs the edge of the cigarette boat, pulling it closer so he can dump them by my feet.

"We're going to need these."

Several grenades roll past me like eggs that have slipped from their cartoon. My heart stops, waiting for one of them to go off.

"What are you doing?"

Henrik has his back to me, fiddling with something I can't see.

Austin looks down and says, "Holy cow."

"Holy cow what?"

When my brother catches my eye, he looks both excited and nervous. "You're probably not going to like it, but it has to be done."

"What has to be done?"

At this point, I'm thinking the only thing that has to be done is for us to get the hell away from Loch Ness and let the military handle the rest.

Because when I look around, I see we're not alone.

Under slate skies and teeming rain, the shores of the loch are filling with people. Dozens and dozens of people. All of them drawn by the barrage of gunfire and explosions. And quite possibly the unearthly cry of the monsters.

They're gathering around the bodies on land. Everyone seems to have a phone in their hand, aimed at the dead Nessies.

So far, they don't seem to notice us.

I have a feeling that once Henrik is done, that will change in a hurry.

CHAPTER TWENTY-EIGHT

I've never had a migraine before, but I think one is starting to blossom in my skull now. It feels as if someone's trying to pry my cranium apart with a rusty can opener. A burst of nausea hits me so hard, I clamp my hand over my mouth to keep my gorge down.

I don't even know that Henrik and Austin have climbed back on board the cigarette boat.

"There she goes," Austin says.

Through the haze of pain, I see Vindicta cruising out to the deeper part of the loch.

'What did you guys do?"

Henrik cuts the engine of the cigarette boat. "I want your pontoon boat to have their undivided attention."

I look to the shore.

It appears we're starting to get some attention as well. I point our audience out to Austin and Henrik.

Austin deflates. "Damn. We have to get them away from here."

"Short of tear gas and a riot squad, that's not gonna happen. They're standing near the bodies of Loch Ness Monsters. Even those who never believed aren't going to just walk away."

Henrik has a rifle in his hand again, scanning the water for any creatures that decide they'd like to get up close and personal with the onlookers. "We'll all have a lot less to worry about in a little over two minutes."

We see the rising and falling backs of the Loch Ness Monstrosities as they sail toward Vindicta, slithering lake snakes of destruction.

Henrik says, "I'm hoping their intelligence will be their downfall."

Austin grips my hand. "How?"

"At first, they were attracted by the food. As Natalie has stated, the loch is being depleted because of their return, or maturation. But the food is gone and they are still here. Normally, elusive creatures do not go counter to their conditioning. Unless, in this case, they have the intelligence to hate. They want us dead. They will not leave until they've tasted our blood. And they think we're on board Vindicta."

I see something out of the corner of my eye that deadens my soul.

I ask Henrik, "What did you do?"

"I set a time controlled bomb that will go off just about the time they make their attack. And then we can…we can."

He sees it too. Austin squeezes my hand so tight, I momentarily forget the pounding in my head.

"Fucking tourists."

One of the Loch Ness tour boats, a double decker that cruises up and down the loch twice a day, pointing out historic sites and talking about, of course, the monster, is heading right into the trajectory of Vindicta.

I gun the cigarette boat to life and hit the throttle hard.

Henrik stumbles to get next to me. "What are you doing?"

"We can't let Vindicta blow up near that tour boat!"

"How are you going to stop a boat that big?"

"I'm not. We're going to push Vindicta off course."

Austin is now on my other side, the wind and rain slapping our faces. "But you're going to have to ride right into those things to do it!"

"I'd rather that than have all those lives on my conscience."

The Loch Ness Monstrosities are right behind Vindicta, like dogs chasing the mail truck. I can barely hear the loudspeaker on the tour boat, the guide going on about sonar readings of the loch and to be on the lookout for anything mysterious.

If one person spots the approaching creatures, soon they'll all see. And then there will be screaming. I'm glad the cigarette boat's engines are so loud I won't be able to hear them.

I am appreciative of the fact that Henrik isn't talking me out of doing what I know is insane, at least in terms of going against out natural inclination toward self-preservation. Austin is another story. I know he feels the same way. We didn't set out for things to go down like this. Not by a long shot.

Vindicta rolls right along. I can only imagine what Henrik has locked and loaded on her. If he thought he could take most of these things out with it, it must be huge.

The tour boat cleaves through the rocky loch. It's so big, changing course will not be easy. Even if they see the writhing creatures, they won't be able to avoid them or my unmanned boat in time to be spared from the upcoming blast.

"I need you guys to hold on."

I jam the cigarette boat to another gear a second before we enter the pod of beasts. We hit the hump of one and take to the air. I can feel the blades of the engine tear through its flesh.

The boat slams back down. My teeth clack together so hard, I'm sure I've cracked a couple of molars. It reignites the stabbing in my skull. I'm close to passing out.

Shit. Not now.

We ride over the backs of the creatures, going too fast for them to react. I shoot past Vindicta on my left, the tour boat on my right. The captain lets his horn bellow.

"Yeah, I can see you."

I make a tight turn so now we're facing Vindicta and the Loch Ness Monstrosities. There's quite a bit of blood in the water. If Henrik is right, it's only making them madder.

"Now here comes the fun part. Austin, make sure I don't go flying."

He has one hand gripping a rail and now the other around my waist. I look over at Henrik and I think he's praying.

Good. We can use all the help we can get.

I make a beeline for Vindicta. We close the gap in seconds. Our bows glance off one another. The shock is intense, but I hit the angle just right so it's not a deathly head on collision. I can hear the fiberglass of the cigarette boat tear.

Vindicta makes a hard left, now heading way from where she and the tour boat would have collided.

I'm about to give a little victory shout when Vindicta goes boom.

And realize I didn't get us far enough away.

CHAPTER TWENTY-NINE

I'm pretty sure the explosion has shattered my eardrums. There's a brief boom, then a feeling of being kicked in the chest, followed by silence and falling.

For the second time today, I'm thrown from the boat I'm on, and it doesn't get easier with repetition. I don't know whether the cigarette boat has gone to pieces or if a massive swell of water sent us flying in every direction. I see the sky, the tour boat, and hit the water.

I don't want to go through that whole drowning bit again, so I immediately swim for the surface. The moment I pop up, I see Austin just a few feet away. There's a splash, and Henrik has joined the swimming party.

Austin says something. I must not be deaf because I can hear. Of course, what I can hear is a high-pitched ringing, not my brother's voice.

"What?"

I can tell by the look on his face that he's having the same issue. So he points behind me.

The cigarette boat isn't in tiny pieces. But it is taking on water.

Vindicta is nothing but flaming bits o' boat scattered everywhere.

Henrik tugs at me, guiding me to the boat. Austin is right behind us, swimming with sure, broad strokes. Me, I'm struggling to stay afloat. I'm exhausted and hurt and not sure my brain isn't leaking from my useless ears.

I'm suddenly lifted up by Austin and basically tossed onto the boat. I land on my side. I think I have a cracked rib, and this little impact has done wonders for it.

"et...th...uns."

Austin is standing over me.

"I can't hear you."

Wait. I could hear that! My ears are still whining like dog whistles, but something is coming through.

He puts his face inches from mine. "We have to get the guns before she sinks."

"Billy Firth is not going to be happy."

"Huh?"

"Never mind. Help me up." He grabs my hand and pulls. The exertion feels as if I ruptured a lung. I figure I'll be coughing up blood any second now.

The boat tips when Henrik scrambles aboard. "We're surrounded. I think only a couple of them went for your boat. I see pieces of some, but I can't tell how many."

I grab a rifle in my numb hands. "Great. We're on a sinking ship surrounded by vengeful animals. You think they're smart enough to know what a white flag means?"

There's no humor in Henrik's eyes. For the first time, the thick ice of his cool demeanor is cracking. "No."

Austin pulls the pin on a grenade and launches it toward one of the creatures circling the boat. "Good, because we don't have anything white aboard."

The grenade detonates, there's a plume of scarlet water and the others retreat, but only for a moment.

"How many more of those have we got?"

Henrik does a quick count. "Nine."

I sigh and it hurts like hell. "I was hoping you'd say a hundred. Look, we have to get off this boat or we'll be in the water with those things in about five minutes." I start waving my arms at the tour boat. There's a return bleat of the horn. They see, and they're coming. Everyone has moved to the front of the boat to watch the carnage.

The Loch Ness Monstrosities regroup and head back for us. Damn, they really do hate our guts.

It's mutual.

I guess I can't blame them, considering how much of their brethren's guts are bobbing on the water.

Austin tosses another grenade and they scatter. This time when it goes off, it does so impotently. They learn awfully fast.

"They're not making this easy."

Austin has pulled the pin of another. His arm is cocked back and he's ready to throw at a moment's notice. "It's not killing them, but it is scaring them off. We can use what we have left to keep them from attacking the tour boat once they pick us up."

He's got a point. I'm too fucked up to think straight.

"Here they come," Henrik says.

The tour boat slips next to us just as the water has come to our knees. Two of the mates throw a ladder down the side of the boat and shout for us to get on board quickly. They keep glancing at the gathering of monsters.

Austin practically launches me onto the tour boat. I'm surrounded by people asking a thousand questions I don't feel like answering.

He's on board next, still gripping the live grenade, three rifles slung over his shoulder.

Henrik goes for the ladder and slips. He flops into the water.

Austin lets the rifles slide off his shoulder. They clatter on the deck, eliciting some terrified screams from the crowd. Do they think we've gone through all of this just to shoot them?

He leans over the side of the boat. "Take my hand!"

Whatever weapons Henrik had hoped to save are now sinking fast. The monsters, sensing one of the focuses of their ire is vulnerable, speed toward him.

One of them was swimming too deep for us to see. It comes up under Henrik, launching him in the air. Somehow, Austin snags his arm, and then they're both flipping end over end.

The grenade falls from his grasp, landing on the deck of the tour boat.

I scream, "Everybody get the hell away! Go! Go! Go!"

There's a collective shout of terror and a stampeded to the other side of the boat.

I try to kick the grenade overboard before I join them, but it just bounces against the lip. When it goes off, the tour boat rocks to one side, to the point where I think it's going to tip over.

Everyone is in a panic. I muscle my way through the crowd, rushing back to the other side to look for my brother and Henrik.

They're gone.

CHAPTER THIRTY

I'm too dazed to cry, too numb to even shout their names until my throat is raw.

The creatures are battering the tour boat. The air is filled with desperate screams.

And nowhere in any of the madness is my twin brother. Or Henrik.

Keeping in line with my current role as harbinger of death to anything aquatic, the tour boat is now listing to one side, the damage from the grenade fatal. I see the captain is heading for land, carving through the creatures who simply snap at the ship and hurl their bodies against the hull.

They know I'm here.

They won't stop until I join Austin and Henrik.

I look back. There are children on board – wide-eyed, frightened boys and girls. I even spot a baby in a stroller, her mother staring out at the loch with an uncomprehending gaze.

We're not going to make it. The ship is really struggling. When the captain eventually calls to abandon ship and people take to the lifeboats, it will only make easier pickings for the Nessies.

Unless.

Unless.

I step over the rail. No one is paying attention to me. I bet they've even forgotten I was the person shooting at these things who blew up her own boat. I'm the one who invited death to their tour.

A monster spots me and takes a swipe at me with its tail, just missing my legs. I don't move a muscle. Let it have me if it wants me. If I give them what they crave, maybe the innocents aboard the tour boat will live.

My body starts to sway as the ship limps along. I'm going to fall any second now.

And I'm fine with it.

A hideous face pokes out of the water just below me. If Satan had an aquarium, that would be the face looking at me on the other side of the glass. I don't know what the hell these things are. I'll never know. But I know what they did to me. And now they know what I did to them.

Time to end it.

"Nat!"

I reach back to grab the handrail.

"Austin!"

He's treading water. He's firing a Bullpup rifle just under the water. A stream of bubbles is left in the wake of each round. Somehow, he's managed to clear a path to the ship. Henrik is right beside him, looking pale as death.

"Help me up!" Austin roars. "I'm running out of ammo!"

I find a life preserver that's tethered to the ship and toss it down. I don't know if I have the strength to pull them up. Austin is double my weight and then some.

"I need help!" I scream. One of the mates, a young guy with longish hair and an oozing pimple on the end of his nose, rushes to my side. "We have to get them out of there."

He turns his head and barks, "Ey, come over here!"

Another mate, this one not much older but broad as a barn, reaches to grab the rope.

"Just hold on, Austin."

Austin has to drop the rifle in order to grab on to the life preserver with one arm and Henrik with the other. It's a struggle, but we do get them on board, collapsing in a wet, heaving heap.

"I thought you…"

Austin flashes a tired smile. "Yeah, me too. Good thing Henrik didn't drop everything." He looks over at the gaping, charred hole in the ship. "Crap, did I do that?"

I shake my head. "No. The grenade did. Henrik, are you all right?"

His side is lacerated and leaking blood. He presses down on it with a slight groan. "Nothing some stitches can't fix."

Our happy reunion is cut short by a barrage of shrieks on the other side of the tour boat.

We get up to see.

One of the monsters managed to make its way onto the deck. It has a woman in its jaws, shaking her back and forth violently. I hear something crack like dry tinder. My stomach turns when I realize it's her spine breaking in half.

Its tail swishes back and forth, taking people's feet out from under them. It drops the woman and heads for a man blubbering on his back, hands held out as if they were an impenetrable shield.

I can't take any more.

I hear some kind of wounded animal cry. It takes me a moment to realize it's coming from me.

My feet are moving on their own. Not sure my brain is in charge anymore. I spy an oar hanging on a wall, grab it, and rush the monster. It lifts its ugly head to stare right at me. I smash the oar right into its unsightly mug.

The blow stuns the creature long enough for everyone to get out of the immediate area.

I look at the end of the oar and it sheared right off. Hell of a shot. And now it's even better because it's all sharp splinters.

The monster lunges for me, but I skip out of the way, knowing the tail is coming next, which I hop over as it whooshes under my feet.

"That's right, we can learn, too!"

I try to stab its side with the broken oar, but it can't penetrate the thick skin.

I'm off balance. The Loch Ness Monstrosity goes for my side. I feel its teeth pinch my flesh.

Oh God it hurts.

"Get...the fuck...off her!"

Austin is punching it in the face as if he were in a boxing ring. I don't know if he's hurting it, but he sure has it confused. It lets me go. I fall to my hands and knees.

Add a punctured spleen to the list.

Henrik is limping over. "Can you hold it by the neck?"

I know he can't be talking to me.

Austin wraps it in a headlock. It lifts him off his feet.

Henrik waits for it to set Austin back down. When it does, I see he has a handgun. He quickly shoves the barrel in the creature's eye and pulls the trigger.

It dies instantly.

"So, that's all we had to do?" I mutter.

The steady thumping of the creatures against the ailing tour boat sets my teeth on edge. They're going to reduce it to kindling way before it sinks from the grenade's blast hole.

I look to Austin. "Okay, what's next?"

"I'm all out of ideas."

"And I'm out of weapons," Henrik says, tossing the handgun down.

"There can't be many more."

Henrik shakes his head. He's shivering. Shock must be settling in. "Four. Maybe five."

"Do we just give them what they want?"

Austin puffs up. "Hell no."

"But the kids…"

"We'll figure something out."

"We don't have much time."

Henrik slumps next to me. Blood is oozing between his fingers plastered to his side. "We're not going to make land. It will be close, but close won't save us."

Austin helps me stagger to the bow. It's so close. I can see the crowds and the dead Nessies. There must be hundreds of people now. Word spreads fast in the Highlands, even without phones or social media.

There are police and ambulances there, too. I can just make out their flashing lights.

We'll have some 'splaining to do.

Or, if we survive – which is a big fat if – maybe we can just melt into the crowd and make our escape.

But we need medical attention. And with that will come questions. People will finger us as the folks who brought an arsenal to stir up the creatures in the loch.

The remaining creatures know where we're headed and have made a barrier of themselves between us and land. Christ on a cracker.

I look to my brother. Nothing has turned out the way we planned it. And if Henrik wasn't here, we would have been dead ten times over.

If we go by the eye for an eye philosophy, I'd say we've come out on top. Twenty of those things for my mother and father. Still, I want more.

"Well, this is it. McQueen's last stand." I look around for a weapon and see only scared people.

Austin is lost in thought, biting his lower lip like it's a cheap steak.

The ship's engines suddenly die.

The monsters raise their heads from the water in a synchronized moment of bowel emptying terror.

I'd brace myself, but my body hurts too much to hold the tension.

We drift into their midst. We'll be right where they want us in five seconds.

Four

Three

Two

O...

CHAPTER THIRTY-ONE

Rob Rayman storms the shore with the assault rifle in his hands, looking like Rambo if Rambo was older and an accountant with a score to settle.

The creatures, their long necks and heads exposed, clumped close together, have made themselves an ideal target.

I yank on Austin's arm and pull him down to the deck. I turn back to everyone behind us and order them to do the same.

Then the shooting starts. Bullets zip overhead, burrow holes into the ship.

All I can hear is otherworldly shrieking and the crash of water. People on the boat and shore scream for their lives.

And then it stops.

The tour boat continues its lazy but steady course to shallow water.

There's a roar of applause, then cheering.

Austin and I barely manage to stand. The crowd on the shore has surrounded Rob and lifted them on their shoulders. He's being paraded around like a conquering hero.

I look over the side of the ship.

The heads of the beasts have been separated from their necks, bobbing on the water like rotten apples.

Rob deserves all of their accolades. He's a true blue hero.

He sees me and winks. Not only will he have the best footage of the most insane battle between man and nature, but he'll also be the man who conquered the mythic, saving dozens, if not hundreds, of people.

I bet he's glad he came over to my RV now.

None of our wounds are as bad as they feel. They stitch Henrik right up in the ambulance. I'm told I have to go to the hospital for X-rays. I promise them I will, on my own, soon. There's so much going on, I just walk out of the ambulance and find Austin. He's watching TV crews interview Rob.

"I got to him before they came," he says. "Made him promise not to say a word about us. You think he's good for it?"

"Yep. He's going to be famous. People will make movies about him."

Austin shakes his head. "You think once he settles down and all of this shit sinks in that he'll be able to live with himself, knowing he killed the creatures he only wanted to prove existed?"

Rob is beaming into a camera. There's a fresh bandage wrapped around his head and his face is covered in tan Band-Aids. Someone was nice enough to clean the blood off of him. There are over a dozen microphones in his face. It's a freaking melee. You'd think George Clooney just dropped in to announce he was running for president.

Rob Rayman. I never would have pegged him for a hero. If anything, I thought I'd be the one saving *his* life. The more I know, the more I realize I don't know jack shit.

I tug on Austin's arm. "Come on. We should find Henrik and get out of here before people start to question us."

"No need to go very far."

Henrik has a big bandage around his waist. He looks a little better, which is a shade less than death.

"I made a go bag before we left. I just need to stop at my RV, grab it, and we can get in your nondescript pink van and vamoose."

In for a penny, in for a hundred pounds, we spot a running car, its occupants part of the throng, jump inside and take off. There's no way we could walk back to my RV. Not in the shape we're in. We leave the car on the main road so it'll be easy to find.

I grab my go bag and Austin gathers his stuff. We throw it in the back of Henrik's van. I run my fingers over the painted rainbow.

Yep. No one will suspect a trio of monster killers are in this puppy.

Henrik is at the wheel. He looks like he'd rather be sleeping. "I mapped out an escape route. There's a safe place for us to stay a little over an hour from here. That's about all I have left in me right now."

Austin sits in the front, next to him. "I hope I have that much, buddy."

We drive away. I wave goodbye to my VW Bug. "So long, Eileen. I hope someone nice adopts you."

I can't help shedding a few tears as I watch my former life disappear, wondering if anyone besides Mrs. Carr will really miss me.

"Henrik, I can't thank you for all you've done. We wouldn't have made it through all of that without you." I rest my hand on his narrow shoulder.

"I'm glad I could help."

Without Henrik and Rob, all of those years of anticipation and plotting ways to exact our revenge would have come to nothing but our deaths. I guess I'm not the badass I pretend to be. Maybe it's something about Austin and me. We attract trouble. Except this time, we had good people to pull our asses from the fire.

The rain isn't letting up. The wipers are working overtime.

Isn't rain supposed to stop at moments like this?

Hollywood, this isn't.

"Pull in over there," I say.

Austin looks at me as if I've lost the few marbles I have left. "We have to get the hell out of here."

"We're fine for now. Everyone is down at the Loch. It'll only take a couple of minutes."

I dash out into the rain. The bell above the door tinkles. I have to get real close before Mrs. Carr recognizes me.

"Oh my, dearie. Have you heard about the commotion?"

"There's a commotion?"

Her hand flutters to her mouth. There's a big smile on her face. "They say they caught the creature."

"You mean Nessie?"

"The one and only. Isn't that wonderful?"

It's safe to assume she doesn't know Nessie is a bunch of creatures and they've been slaughtered.

"Now we can show the world we weren't out of our heads, that's right."

I reach out and pat her hand. "It sure is." I shock her by kissing her cheek.

"Now that's two surprises in one day."

"I just wanted to thank you for always looking out for me. And speaking of that, do you still have that box of books?"

She's rooted to the spot for a few moments, I think more stunned by my kiss than the discovery of Nessie. "Ah, yes, yes, right over there, behind the mops and buckets."

I let her know I've got it before she tries to scoot out from behind the counter and lift it.

"How much for all of the books?"

"You might now want to read all of them, dearie."

"No matter. I like options."

"Just take them. I'm in a celebrating mood today."

I lay a hundred pound note on the counter, out of her line of sight. "Thanks again, Mrs. Carr. If they found Nessie, I expect you're going to be very busy for a while. Celebrate while you can."

"Oh, I will. How was Billy Firth's boat?"

That makes me cringe. I have to anonymously send him a load of cash to pay for his boat which is now on the bottom of the loch. Make it double.

"It was great. Just what I needed."

The bell tinkles again as I leave. The rain pelts the closed cardboard box.

"Can we actually go now?" Austin says.

"Yes, yes. Hit the road."

The van fishtails in the mud and we're off.

After twenty minutes of driving in numb silence, Henrik says, "I think it's best we take a few months to recuperate. We'll need to restore our strength. And I don't mean just physically. I have a wonderful place in mind. You'll both love it."

Austin says, "I don't care where it is, as long as it has a comfortable bed. I plan to sleep for a month."

My own eyelids are heavier than bank vaults. "Some R&R sounds good to me."

Henrik smiles. "And I'll teach you all you need to know about where we're going in Indonesia. We won't have to worry about being found out by the locals, unless you're concerned about being seen by monkeys."

Indonesia.

Orang Pendeks.

I'm too damn tired to worry about it.

Sighing, I open the box lid and sputter with laughter. The book at the very top is a yellowed copy of *Jaws*.

Cradling the book to my chest, I lean back in the seat and close my eyes.

So I sleep, and hope this time, if I see my parents in my dreams, we can sit and talk and enjoy our company. It would be really, really nice to hear the sound of their voices.

THE END

Hunter Shea is the product of a misspent childhood watching scary movies, reading forbidden books and wishing Bigfoot would walk past his house. He doesn't just write about the paranormal – he actively seeks out the things that scare the hell out of people and experiences them for himself. Hunter's novels can even be found on display at the International Cryptozoology Museum. The Montauk Monster was named one of the best reads of the summer by Publishers Weekly. Not since Dr. Frankenstein has someone been as dedicated to making monsters, penning such titles as The Jersey Devil, They Rise, Swamp Monster Massacre and The Dover Demon. His video podcast, Monster Men, is one of the most watched horror podcasts in the world. Living with his wonderful family and two cats, he's happy to be close enough to New York City to gobble down Gray's Papaya hotdogs when the craving hits. You can follow his madness at

www.huntershea.com.

 SEVEREDPRESS

CHECK OUT OTHER GREAT DEEP SEA THRILLERS

MEGA
by Jake Bible

There is something in the deep. Something large. Something hungry. Something prehistoric.
And Team Grendel must find it, fight it, and kill it.
Kinsey Thorne, the first female US Navy SEAL candidate has hit rock bottom. Having washed out of the Navy, she turned to every drink and drug she could get her hands on. Until her father and cousins, all ex-Navy SEALS themselves, offer her a way back into the life: as part of a private, elite combat Team being put together to find and hunt down an impossible monster in the Indian Ocean. Kinsey has a second chance, but can she live through it?

THE BLACK
by Paul E Cooley

Under 30,000 feet of water, the exploration rig Leaguer has discovered an oil field larger than Saudi Arabia, with oil so sweet and pure, nations would go to war for the rights to it. But as the team starts drilling exploration well after exploration well in their race to claim the sweet crude, a deep rumbling beneath the ocean floor shakes them all to their core. Something has been living in the oil and it's about to give birth to the greatest threat humanity has ever seen.

"The Black" is a techno/horror-thriller that puts the horror and action of movies such as Leviathan and The Thing right into readers' hands. Ocean exploration will never be the same."

CHECK OUT OTHER GREAT
DEEP SEA THRILLERS

PREDATOR X
by C.J Waller

When deep level oil fracking uncovers a vast subterranean sea, a crack team of cavers and scientists are sent down to investigate. Upon their arrival, they disappear without a trace. A second team, including sedimentologist Dr Megan Stoker, are ordered to seek out Alpha Team and report back their findings. But Alpha team are nowhere to be found – instead, they are faced with something unexpected in the depths. Something ancient. Something huge. Something dangerous. Predator X

DEAD BAIT
by Tim Curran

A husband hell-bent on revenge hunts a Wereshark...A Russian mail order bride with a fishy secret...Crabs with a collective consciousness...A vampire who transforms into a Candiru...Zombie piranha...Bait that will have you crawling out of your skin and more. Drawing on horror, humor with a helping of dark fantasy and a touch of deviance, these 19 contemporary stories pay homage to the monsters that lurk in the murky waters of our imaginations. If you thought it was safe to go back in the water...Think Again!

CHECK OUT OTHER GREAT
DEEP SEA THRILLERS

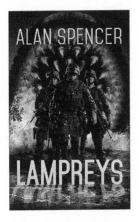

LAMPREYS
by Alan Spencer

A secret government tactical team is sent to perform a clean sweep of a private research installation. Horrible atrocities lurk within the abandoned corridors. Mutated sea creatures with insane killing abilities are waiting to suck the blood and meat from their prey.
Unemployed college professor Conrad Garfield is forced to assist and is soon separated from the team. Alone and afraid, Conrad must use his wits to battle mutated lampreys, infected scientists and go head-to-head with the biggest monstrosity of all.
Can Conrad survive, or will the deadly monsters suck the very life from his body?

DEEP DEVOTION
by M.C. Norris

Rising from the depths, a mind-bending monster unleashes a wave of terror across the American heartland. Kate Browning, a Kansas City EMT confronts her paralyzing fear of water when she traces the source of a deadly parasitic affliction to the Gulf of Mexico. Cooperating with a marine biologist, she travels to Florida in an effort to save the life of one very special patient, but the source of the epidemic happens to be the nest of a terrifying monster, one that last rose from the depths to annihilate the lost continent of Atlantis.

Leviathan, destroyer, devoted lifemate and parent, the abomination is not going to take the extermination of its brood well.

Made in the USA
San Bernardino, CA
21 January 2017